T0156572

THE DAY
MOYSHE TUSHMAN
BECAME A FOUNTAIN PEN

THE DAY
MOYSHE TUSHMAN
BECAME A FOUNTAIN PEN

A Humorous Novel

BARON Z. HALPERN

THE DAY MOYSHE TUSHMAN BECAME A FOUNTAIN PEN

iUniverse books may be ordered through booksellers or by contacting:

iUniverse
1663 Liberty Drive
Bloomington, IN 47403
www.iuniverse.com
1-800-Authors (1-800-288-4677)

Because of the dynamic nature of the Internet, any web addresses or links contained in this book may have changed since publication and may no longer be valid. The views expressed in this work are solely those of the author and do not necessarily reflect the views of the publisher, and the publisher hereby disclaims any responsibility for them.

Any people depicted in stock imagery provided by Thinkstock are models, and such images are being used for illustrative purposes only. Certain stock imagery © Thinkstock.

ISBN: 978-1-4917-8492-1 (sc)
ISBN: 978-1-4917-8493-8 (e)

Library of Congress Control Number: 2015920287

Print information available on the last page.

iUniverse rev. date: 12/09/2015

Dedicated to my loving wife Barbara for her unfaltering love and devotion throughout our 49 years of marriage

PROLOGUE

The Tushman family name was Zitsontush until Herman Zitsontush changed it to Tushman when he arrived in America..

Moyshe Tushman is a fourth generation American Mensche.

Moyshe's ancestors lived in Bupkis, Europe. They observed *Mensche* Religion. *Mensche Observers* were constantly being annoyed by *Nudniks* (non believers). Annoyance was not the reason that Herman Zitsontush left Bupkis to settle in America. His wife Chutzpah was a constant nag. That was the reason he emigrated from Bupkis in 1893.

Moyshe enlightens us with his perception of birth. We learn about several traditions that are observed by followers of Mensche Religion. Several events occurred during Moyshe's very early childhood that affected his life.

We meet *Bubby* Rifka. She was the woman that had the most influence on his understanding of life. She answered many questions that Moyshe's parents refused to answer.

We are surprised to find out that Moyshe's Paternal Ancestors had a substantial influence on the outcome of European history.

Moysche is in search of his "Mission in Life". His "Mission" was to become a "Fountain Pen". His "Mission in Life" started when he was in Elementary School. We read about and envision his experiences as he travels the very long road to accomplish his "Mission".

HERE COME'S MOYSHE

CHAPTER I

MOYSHE TUSHMAN KNEW FROM WHERE HE CAME

Moyshe recalls "I had been floating in a sea of warm water for approximately nine months. The water was enclosed in a dark cave that had soft fleshy walls. A curled up rope anchored to the back wall of the cave was attached to my belly. Was I being held as a prisoner?

The cave kept growing as days, weeks and months passed. During the 6th month, the walls swelled so much that I couldn't see the ceiling. Every time I stretched my legs to do a frog kick to swim, I could faintly hear my mother say "Michael come feel the baby kicking".

At the end of the ninth month, the cave kept getting larger, then smaller, then larger. My mother called the movement "contractions". The space closed around me whenever I yawned and stretched my arms and legs. One evening during the ninth month, the water began to flow rapidly downstream. I flowed with it. I tried to swim upstream to avoid falling out of a hole in the cave. The current was too strong.

My father and mother panicked. The murky water soaked through her white fancy silk panties. The water formed a puddle on the dark brown plush carpet floor. Although I was still in my mother's womb, I had a good sense of everything that was happening. My eye sight was 20/20. My hearing was perfect because my ears were large and the eardrums developed rapidly. I must have been like Super girl. I was able to see and hear through the thick walls of my mother's stomach. My father speed dialed the pink princess style phone. He spoke to a man named Doctor Max.

Then my father went to the kitchen. He opened a door that was located under the kitchen sink. He bent over and he put his hand into the compartment that was behind the door. He grabbed a small brown paper lunch bag.

My father put my mother's white night gown, white panties and blue slippers into the bag. My mother was upset. She insisted that her outfit should match. My father reached into the small brown lunch bag and took the blue slippers out of the bag. He threw the blue slippers onto the floor. He rushed to their bedroom to get my mother's white slippers. She was satisfied that he had the white slippers in his hand. My father put the white slippers into the small brown lunch bag.

Then he carried the bag in his left hand and held my mother's left arm with his right hand. He rushed her through the large 14'x14' living room and a short 3' length hallway. The hallway was 18" wide. The Living room floor was covered with a plush dark green carpet. The walls were covered with wallpaper. The wallpaper had a dark green background with a blue and yellow flowers print. The hallway had a dark oak hardwood floor. The walls were covered with wallpaper. The wallpaper had a dark blue background with a pink and yellow flowers print. A dark oak stained door opened to the outside. My mother opened the door because my father's hands trebled with fear and he couldn't grab the door handle. My mother was calm, cool and collected by the time that they reached the front door.

She had no trouble grabbing the door knob. She was able to open the door and hold it open for my father. They hobbled down the dark gray painted five porch steps on to a black asphalt 5' pathway that led to a gray concrete sidewalk.

The morning sun was bright enough to light the way. My father put the small brown lunch bag into the trunk of a light blue four door car. The light blue four door car had four whitewall tires. My mother screamed at my father. He left her standing at the back door of the four door light blue car that had four whitewall tires.

My father took the small brown lunch bag out of the trunk. He scurried back to my mother. She screamed "why did you take the small brown lunch bag out of the trunk of the light blue four door car?" He grabbed her *tush* (ass) and shoved her into the back seat of the car.

I was concerned that we were going to have an accident because my father drove very fast. I heard a siren sound. There was a red light flashing on the top of a black and white car.

The man that drove the black and white car with red lights flashing on the roof of the car stopped my father for speeding. A policeman that was dressed in a dark blue outfit stepped out of the black and white car. He looked into the left side front door window. My father opened his window. The policeman leaned over and stuck his head into the open window. He told my father that he stopped the car because my father was speeding. My father explained that he was driving his wife to the hospital because she was pregnant and her water had broken. He had to get to the hospital fast because her contractions were coming every 30 minutes

The policeman told my father that he would only give my father a warning, not a traffic ticket. He told my father to follow him to Women and Children Hospital.

I heard the same loud siren sound. It blasted from the black and white car. My father followed the police car. He drove faster than he did before the encounter with the policeman.

We arrived at the hospital. I could hear a woman tell my parents to look for a man that was dressed in a light blue outfit. He could help my mother hop onto a gurney. My mother noticed that the man also wore a light blue cap on his head and light blue rubber gloves on his hands. My mother was happy that his clothes, gloves and hat were color coordinated.

Less than two minutes later my mother was lying on a gurney inside a bright white room. Another man that was dressed in the exact same color outfit as the other man came into the room and apologized for being late.

He told the other people in the room that he had to help the woman's husband get off the floor. My father had fainted from the odor in the hospital. My mother was in pain. She was still lying on her back atop the gurney. The men in blue placed their arms under her back. The first man in blue counted to three. The two men dressed in blue lifted her up and placed her on a bed. The gurney was three feet away from the bed. It took eight minutes to get her into the bed. The bed was covered with a heavy weight clean white linen sheet. The men in blue left the room.

My mother's legs were covered with a light weight clean white linen sheet. Her legs were partially raised and spread apart. Her feet were firmly pressed onto the bed.

A deep voice said "push". I pushed. The deep voice said "don't push". I stopped pushing. I heard "push one more time". I pushed one more time. I heard several loud screams that came out of the mouth of the woman that was lying on the bed. The woman was my mother. She was crying "I can't push any more" .I floated through a tunnel toward a tiny hole until a bright light appeared. I realized at that time, that the deep voice was not meant for me to push. It was not my responsibility to push. I fell out of the tunnel. I was spiraling toward the floor until a man caught me. He wore thick, wide, black rimmed eye glasses. He was wearing white latex gloves on his hands. He wore a white mask that covered his mouth. His white gown and white cap matched his white mask. My mother was happy that his entire outfit was color coordinated. The man held me upside down and he spanked me. He continually spanked me until I cried. My *tush* hurt from the spanking. The mean man that spanked me was Doctor Max.

I was out of the cave. It felt good that I was able to stretch my arms and legs. There was nothing around me except fresh air. Everyone in the room appeared to be pleased that I was crying. Although the spanking hurt me, they didn't seem to care! I was still hanging upside down. I opened my eyes. I was able to see a calendar hanging on a white color wall. The white calendar had a red colored circle drawn around a date. The black printed date was Tuesday, February 29. 1944. It was a leap year.

A woman named Nurse Nancy declared, "that was an easy birth. The baby's mother was in labor for only eighteen hours". My father thought that Nurse Nancy was confused. How could the labor last eighteen hours? My mother's contractions were 30 minutes apart. Nurse Nancy was short and chunky. She had large chubby fingers that extended from her large chubby hands. Nurse Nancy was dressed in an all white outfit. She wore white shoes and a white cap. My mother was happy that Nurse Nancy's outfit was color coordinated.

Nurse Nancy grabbed me out of Doctor Max's hands and she carried me to a silver metal sink. She washed me from head to toe with cold soapy water. Although she used baby non tear liquid soap, my eyes did sting. After drying me with a clean white, soft terry cloth towel, she placed me on a silver metal table. The table was covered with a clean white linen sheet. Nurse Nancy reached into her pocket and took a long thin object out of her pocket. It was made of clear glass and it had small numbers and lines written on the outside. Someone called it a thermometer.

I was lying on my back. Nurse Nancy held my legs up in the air. She held my feet in her left hand while she held the thermometer in her right hand. She held the thermometer at a ninety degree angle. Nurse Nancy jammed the glass thermometer into *my tush.* The thick ball-shaped silver metal end came in first. I did not enjoy it. I guess that I was lucky. It was not a hockey stick.

I cried "*Oy vey*" (woe is me)! Lucky for me, the glass did not shatter inside my *tush*. I shuddered every time Nurse Nancy came near me.

I got even with her. The next time that she held my legs up in the air, I peed upward into her face. Lucky for her, she wore thick glasses. After that incident, she approached me with caution.

I thought to myself "Next time please *kish mien tush* (kiss my ass) instead of jamming me with the torpedo". The next time she approached me I had fear in my head. I looked at her right hand. "*Got Tzu Gaten*" (Thank Supreme Being). She was not holding the torpedo. Nurse Nancy put a diaper on me and wrapped me in a clean, white, soft cloth blanket with blue stripes.

Nurse Nancy picked me up. She knew that I could not walk so she carried me to my mother.

The first thing that my mother did was to check my entire body. She said to my father that I was definitely his son because I had a small *schmeckle (penis)*. I was definitely a descendant of Adam and Eva Zitsontush. My *tush* was covered with pimples.

My mother counted my fingers and toes. There were five fingers on each hand and five toes on each foot. It really tickled as her pointer finger touched each one of my toes and fingers. She exclaimed sobbing with tears of joy "*Got Tzu Gaten!*" there are ten fingers and ten toes. They must have been expecting to count ten fingers and ten toes.

My mother held me tight against her soft smooth round-shaped boobs. I thought that I was lying atop a mountain. If she did not hold me tight I could have fallen off. I would have to latch onto one of her kinipples so that I wouldn't fall off. Maybe I should have practiced falling because I liked hanging onto her kinipples.

I looked around the room. Doctor Max was standing at the foot of the bed where I was first introduced to him. My father was on the left side of the bed squeezing my mother's hand. His knuckles were whiter than a ghost. He had a huge smile that stretched from ear to ear. I saw a small tear flow from the side of his left eye onto his left cheek. Did the tear mean that he was disappointed that I was a boy? Nurse Nancy was standing on the right side of the bed. She was preparing a bottle into which she poured a milky white color fluid. It was a milky white color because it was milk. It wasn't whole milk. It wasn't 2% milk. It wasn't 1% milk. It wasn't skim milk. Nurse Nancy told my father that my mother refused to breast feed the baby. I certainly would have preferred to kinibble on my mother's kinipples instead of the light brown rubber kinipple that was screwed onto the bottle. I had no say in the matter because I had not learned how to talk yet.

Nurse Nancy gave the bottle to my father. He started to kinibble on the light brown rubber kinipple. He had no idea what to do with the bottle. I believed that it was a natural reaction. See a kinipple and start kinibbling. My father said that it tasted awful. He declared that it needed sugar.

He stopped kinibbling and he handed the bottle to my mother. She moved the light brown rubber kinipple of the bottle softly around my lips. I parted my lips and she jammed the bottle into my mouth.

I started to kinibble on the light brown rubber kinipple. I had learned how to kinibble by watching my father. I thought that the warm milky fluid tasted really good. I didn't believe that it needed sugar. Actually, I did not know any better. I had never tasted milk before and I had never tasted sugar before. I continued to kinibble until the bottle was empty. My belly hurt because I kinibbled air from the empty bottle.

The next few days I was lying on my back in a cage that was surrounded by four clear plastic walls. There was a blue card attached to the wall closest to my head. I was able to read

"Baby Boy Tushman"
"Weight 24 lb. 15 oz."
"Height 32 inches"

There were several other babies in the room lying on their backs in their own clear plastic cages. I couldn't get any sleep. Every baby in the room cried all day and all night. I cried all day and all night. We all stayed awake all day and all night. I cried out loud in baby talk telling them to shut up. I was the last baby that was brought into the room so I must have been the youngest. No wonder they didn't obey me! The room was called a nursery, probably because there were so many Nurses in the room. Nurses worked in pairs. They continually checked on the babies. I found it interesting that every baby stopped crying when their nurse took them out of their cages to hold them and shove a bottle into their mouths.

The noise became louder. It was not from the crying. The loud noise was caused by the kinibbling on the light brown kinipples that were screwed onto the tops of the bottles. When all babies stopped kinibbling, the loud sound stopped. The next loud sounds were caused by the crying. The crying became louder when the nurses put us back into our cages.

I began to smell a terrible odor. It came from me and the four babies in the cages that were surrounding my cage. The odor became worse. Every baby in the room was pooping. Nurse Nancy picked me up and placed me on to the cold silver steel table. She held my feet up into the air with her left hand. She cleaned my tush and poured a white powder on my stomach, back and *tush.* Then she jammed the thermometer into my *tush!* It was the same routine every two hours. I feared and hated Nurse Nancy. I tried to pee in her face. Nothing came out of my *schmeckle.* It was dry because I had peed all night. Every nurse cleaned the baby that they had the responsibility to clean. The babies really smelled good so the nurses put a brand new diaper on each one of the babies. The nurse next to Nurse Nancy remarked; "they sure do poop a lot".

Nurse Nancy washed the poop out of her manicured finger nails. She did not say a word. She did not laugh!

With the babies' legs in the air, I noticed that some babies had a *schmeckle.* Some of the babies did not have a *schmeckle.* I had a *schmeckle!* It did not take a long time for me to realize that boys have *schmeckles. Girls* do not have *schmeckles!*

Babies with *schmeckles* were dressed in blue onesies They were boys. The babies without *schmeckles* were dressed in pink. They were girls. I wondered what happened to the girls' *schmeckles*. Were they cut off at birth or did their father's push so hard that their *schmeckles* fell off when the babies' parents were making babies?"

How did Moyshe know all of these things?

CHAPTER II

HOME FROM THE HOSPITAL

On the third day of my stay in the hospital my father came to the hospital. He came into the nursery and took me out of my cage. He carried me to my mother and placed me on her lap. She was sitting in a wheel chair. I wondered. "Did she have an accident and hurt herself?" A man dressed in blue wheeled my mother to the car. She couldn't walk. My father carried me to the car He was going to drive the same car that he drove to the hospital. I knew it was the same car. It was a light blue car with four doors and there were four white wall tires. I had been out of the womb for three days so I was able to observe that my father was approximately twenty-four years old. He was handsome, approximately 5'7" tall and he was slender. He had curly black hair combed backward with no part. My mother was approximately twenty-one years old. She was pretty with long blonde hair. She was approximately 5' 5"tall and she was slender. Her breasts size was approximately 34C cup. Her breasts were proportionate for her size body. However, they were larger than normal because she just gave birth to me. They were probably still filled with milk. Eventually, her breasts would shrink. I knew all of those details because I was very observant and I heard my parents talking about the shrinkage.

I believed that every measurement was approximate because I had heard that my parents always exaggerated about the size of my mother's breasts. I did not have a tape measure so I could not verify the size of her breasts.

My mother opened the left back door. My father leaned inside the car and strapped me tightly into a blue plaid baby car seat. He pulled the strap around my chest and belly. I couldn't escape from the blue plaid baby car seat. I thought that I was a prisoner. I could not move other than flap my arms in the air as I cried all of the way home.

The baby car seat was held tight by a black nylon belt. It was strapped to the bottom and back of the bench style seat of the light blue car so that it wouldn't move. My father drove the car and my mother sat in the front passenger seat which was on his right side.

My father kept his hands on the steering wheel with his right hand pointed to 2 o'clock. His left hand was pointed to 10 o'clock. His hands must have been glued to the steering wheel. He never changed their position. My father never said a word. My mother didn't stop talking. She said to my father "I pray to *Supreme Being* that the baby will not be afraid of our "monster" at home." That statement scared me. I wondered, "What kind of monster was waiting at home?" Would it be big, hairy and blue or big, hairy and orange?"

My father did not drive as fast as he did on the way to the hospital. I heard the sound of a siren. My mother looked through the back window. My father looked through his side view and rear view mirror. My mother screamed at my father *"vos Oy mit dir?"* (What's wrong with you)? When we went to the hospital, didn't you learn a lesson not to speed?" My father responded *"kish mien tush,* I was not speeding!" A man dressed in a gray shirt and gray pants dismounted his gray motorcycle. He was wearing a gray hat. My mother was happy that his clothes and hat were color coordinated.

The man was not a policeman. He was a State Trooper. He walked slowly toward our car.

My father rolled down the car window. The State Trooper asked for my father's driver's license and car registration. My father asked why? He knew that he wasn't speeding.

The State Trooper said that the right side of the tail light was not working. My father knew that the tail light wasn't broken. The State Trooper must have been lying. Perhaps he was profiling. My father had a long nose and a dark complexion He looked like a sterotypical *Mensche.* The State Trooper was a Nudnik.

He took both licenses from my father and walked back to his gray motorcycle. He picked up the phone that was attached to the motorcycle. He returned to our car and drew his gun out of its holster as he walked back to our car.

He shouted to my father "put your hands up and hold them outside the car window". The State Trooper stuck his head through my father's window. His gun was still drawn out of the holster. He saw my mother sitting in the front seat and I was strapped into my baby car seat. The trooper told my father to put his hands behind his back and drop to his knees. I thought to myself. "Was this going to be an execution style killing?" My father peed in his pants!

My mother yelled "we're in deep shit". The State Trooper and my father walked back to the car.

My father's hands were clasped behind his back. They were cuffed in a small silver steel contraption. My mother said that the contraption was "hand cuffs. The State Trooper was holding my father's left arm as they walked back to the car. He held my father's head down as he grabbed my *father's tush* and pushed him into the back seat of the car. I began to cry because it was a tight fit. My father was almost on top of me.

Another State Trooper on a motorcycle rode up close to our car. He jumped off the motorcycle and ran toward us. He yelled to the first State Trooper "*Puhtz (*Dick head), release the poor man. The hospital notified us that they have taken an inventory. They were not missing any baby blankets.

The second State Trooper apologized to my father. Nurse Nancy thought that my father had stolen blue striped baby blankets from the hospital. My father didn't say a word. My mother screamed at the State Trooper "go *shtoop* (screw) yourself". The Trooper ran toward my mother. I thought that she was going to get handcuffed! He apologized to my mother. I assumed that he didn't know the English translation for *shtoop*.

My father didn't say a word on the drive home. My mother didn't stop talking.

We arrived home from the hospital. *Got Tzu Gaten (Thank Supreme Being)* I did not see the "monster" that I had pictured in my mind. I heard my mother cry with terror in her voice. She said that my older brother Barney was nowhere to be found. My parents looked throughout the house. They could not find him. I wondered." Did the monster eat my brother or was my brother the monster? Was the monster hiding? Would he eat me?"

The door bell rang. It was the next door neighbor standing at the front door. She was carrying Barney in her hairy, burly arms. She was hunched over as she walked into the house. Everyone in the neighborhood thought that she had a twin brother named "Quasimodo". My parents asked her why she was carrying Barney and where had they been? The old lady cackled as she explained that Barney had told her that he ran away from home because he was very upset.

Barney was expecting to "get" a female blue or green baby parakeet. He did not want a baby brother. I wasn't blue or green. My parents would not trade me for a parakeet. My brother said that he would settle for a yellow canary. They emphatically said "no". That upset Barney more!

The first few days that I was home people were "coming out of the woodwork". They were mostly relatives. They must have read about my birth in the Buffalo *Mensche* Review. Everyone that visited came over to my crib and bent over to put their face close to mine. They were so close that I could smell cigar, cigarette and pipe smoke. Many of them had vodka on their breath. Onions were the worse. They pinched my cheeks and said *"shayna punim"* (a beautiful face). I would have bet, if I was a betting baby that they said *"shana punim"* to all new born babies. However, I must say that I really did have a *shayna punim*.

My 17 years old cousin Oliver leaned over toward me. His face was close to mine. His breath smelled like marijuana. *Got Tzu Gaten* he didn't pinch my cheeks! Oliver was approximately 5'2" tall. He weighed approximately 325 lbs.

After a few days things began to quiet down. My parents agreed that visitation should be by invitation only. Not many people visited because my parents never put postage stamps on the invitations. Only a few people received phone calls inviting them to visit. I was pleased that fewer people visited because it allowed me more sleep time. I needed a lot of sleep time because I did not want to be too tired to play with myself the following day. I did enjoy playing with myself!

My grandmother *Bubby* was thrilled that fewer people came to visit. That gave her a lot of alone time with me. She told me stories whenever we were alone together. I thought that she really believed that I understood her stories, even though I was less than two weeks old!

Bubby enjoyed our alone time. She thought that I was smiling when she told me jokes. She didn't realize that I was smiling because I was passing gas!

My father was a wallpaper hanger. He was working all of the time. My mother went to work with him. She worked part time. Part time was 6 hours, four days a week. She pasted the back of the wallpaper to help him complete the job faster. *Bubby* took care of us when my parents worked or when they went out on a "date". They usually went to see a movie and enjoy a snack after the movie. That was the only exciting thing that they did when they weren't working.

Many other babies told me that their grandmothers sang lullabies to them. *Bubby* never sang to me. Didn't she love me as much as the other grandmothers loved their grandchildren? I found out when I was two years old that she never sang lullabies because she couldn't carry a tune! I was relieved that she didn't sing.

On many occasions, *Bubby* held me on her lap and bounced me up and down. She said "giddy up" as she bounced me. *Bubby* used to get so excited that she bounced me faster. She said "giddy up' louder and bounced me faster until I puked on her. She never learned a lesson. *Bubby* did this daily.

Once in a while my mother pulled me away from *Bubby* and put me on my back to tickle me under my chin. There was many times that *Bubby* got upset with my mother for pulling me away from her. To retaliate she shoved my mother. Several times *Bubby* almost knocked her to the ground. Then *Bubby* would tickle me under the chin and say *shayna punim*. Once in awhile, but not often, my mother shoved back, almost knocking her to the ground.

My father laughed to himself, as he told my mother to stop shoving *Bubby*. He told her that she should punch *Bubby* with closed fists. That irritated *Bubby*. She ran toward my father and punched him with a closed fist. He went into the kitchen and pulled corned beef out of the freezer. He covered his "black and blue eye" with the cold corned beef. *Bubby* was so proud of herself. My mother applauded.

Bubby challenged my mother to dive into a mud pit and wrestle or climb into a boxing ring and slug it out. She suggested that they would not stop until there was a winner. The winner of both contests would play with me Sundays through Thursdays. The loser would play with me on Fridays. They had to rest on Saturdays, the seventh day of the week. Saturday was the *Sabbath. Supreme Being* created the world in six days. He rested on the seventh day. If they tied, they would have to shove each other to get into a good position to play with me first.

It was March 8, 1944, eight days after I was born. It was the day of my"coming out". A big celebration was to begin in a few hours.

BRIT HALIM

A *Brit Halim* is the removal of the foreskin from an eight days old *Mensche* baby boy's *schmeckle* (penis). A *Brit Halim* is actually more than just the procedure of circumcision. It is a ceremony that includes various Mensche traditions and prayers.

My mother dressed me in a dark blue onesie outfit that had snaps on the bottom. It buttoned around my crotch. It's a good thing that I was wearing a thick diaper because my mother could have pinched my *schmeckle* when she buttoned the snaps. My father put a dark blue round *"hapik"* (skull cap) on his own head. He wore a dark blue shirt, dark blue pants and dark blue socks. He put a dark blue hapik on Barney's head. Barney wore a dark blue shirt, dark blue pants and dark blue socks. My father put a small dark blue *hapik* on my head. My mother wore a dark blue dress. *Bubby* wore a dark blue dress. My mother wasn't happy. She was thrilled. We were color coordinated.

I whimpered because my brother Barney kept licking my face and squeezing my fingers when no one was looking. Fortunately for me, *Bubby* came into the room to check on me every three minutes.

She was very protective. The moment that *Bubby* entered the room Barney stopped licking and squeezing. She was my savior!

Bubby was forty years older than my mother. She was a short frumpy woman with salt and pepper shoulder length hair. She was always dressed in a light gray and blue paisley design housedress, except for the day of my *Brit Halim*. She wore black shoes with wide toes and wide very short heels. The wide black shoe laces were frayed at both ends. They were knotted together where they had broken.

There was a loud tumult occurring in the living room not far from my bedroom. I could hear loud voices. The voices were cackling sounds of old biddies. My aunts were the old biddies. I could hear the pitter-patter of children's shoes on the dark oak stain hardwood floor. The hardwood floor led from the dark green plush carpet in the living room to the dark green short plush carpet in my bedroom. The pitter-patter sounds became louder as they approached my bedroom. It was my older twin cousins Mickey and Minerva running around the house. The twins had light blue eyes and light blonde hair. They were tall for their age. My Uncle Donald had brown hair and brown eyes. He worked every Monday through Friday afternoon. My Aunt Dorothy had brown hair and black eyes. The ice cream man that drove around the neighborhood every Monday through Friday afternoon had light blonde hair and light blue eyes. My cousins were three years old. The ice cream man began his route three years prior to their birth. My uncle was short and he had a flabby stomach. Aunt Dorothy always complained that he ate too much and that he never exercised. The ice cream man was tall. His stomach was flat. He boasted about his light blonde hair and light blue eyes. Family members always joked that the twins did not look like my uncle or the milk man. They looked like the ice cream man!

My Aunt Dorothy yelled at the twins to stop jumping on the new white couch. She told them to remove their shoes if they were going to keep jumping. My mother was peeved! Mickey kept jumping from the ottoman to the couch. He fell two times on top of my Brother Barney's head. That was satisfying to me. Many friends of my parents, my aunts and my uncles stood in the living room gabbing with each other. They could not sit because there were no chairs. Mickey and Minerva were busy jumping on the couch and the ottoman so nobody could sit on the couch and the ottoman. Every person in the house was invited to celebrate my *Brit Halim.*

This was my first party. I was so excited because I was to be the center of attention. *"Gantseh Megillah"* (Lucky Me)!

Many medical experts believed that circumcision may prevent disease such as HIV. Circumcision of a *Mensche* boy was "performed" by the Local Butcher. He was trained to "perform" a circumcision. If the Butcher couldn't "perform, it was "performed" by Doctor Max. Most babies wanted Dr. Max to do the circumcision.

Friends and relatives were invited to enjoy watching the cutting of my *schmeckle.* Music started to play The grownups that danced came near me and hopped on one foot as they joined hands to form a circle. They threw miniature tootsie rolls at my head. I was the "center of attention" so they formed a line in order to come up to me. Their faces came close to mine. The only thing that they said was *shayna punim.* They probably didn't have anything else to say. Each one had cigar, cigarette or pipe smoke on their breath. Several people smelled of vodka. My seventeen year old cousin had marijuana on his breath. The guests drank coffee, tea or water. My parents did not serve soda or loganberry.

Grape Manischewitz wine was served during the ceremony. They stuffed their faces with kishka, Nova Scotia lox, tuna fish, eggs and herring. Poppy seed lemon cake and other assorted pastries were the desserts.

The ceremony was about to begin. The *hapik* kept falling off the top of my head. I was lying on my back atop a brand new dark blue silk pillow. My father handed me to my Uncle Theodore. He was my mother's oldest brother. He was the *Kednas* (Honoree). Uncle Theodore had the honor to hold me during the circumcision of my *schmeckle.* He held me until the entire ceremony was completed.

According to Orthodox Mensche tradition, circumcision consisted of three activities.

The three activities included the cutting and removal of the foreskin, pushing the mucous membrane down toward the testicles and finally cleaning of the *schmeckle*.

Uncle Theodore held my feet and spread my legs with his cold hands. *The Local Butcher* was a guest. He held a butcher cleaver in his left hand. He brought his cleaver to every circumcision. He prayed that he would have to stand-in for Dr. Max. Uncle Theodore unsnapped the buttons at the bottom of my onesie. Dr. Max was holding a tiny pair of metal scissors in his right hand and a tiny metal scalpel in his left hand. There was a tiny metal clamp lying on the table. The *Ibbar* said some *Mensche* prayers and the *Rotnac* chanted *some Mensche* hymns as Dr. Max placed the clamp on my *schmeckle.* I panicked and cried as loud as I could. I was hoping that *Bubby* would rescue me *Bubby* did not rescue me. I wished that I knew how to speak Mensche language so that I could scream to her, "save me".

The Local Butcher smiled when Dr. Max clamped me. He told the person next to him that he would have put the clamp on my testicles and my *schmeckle*. Dr. Max cut, snipped and pushed. My *schmeckle* hurt like hell! It bled profusely during the procedure. Dr. Max put some grape Manischewitz wine on a cloth. I sucked on the cloth.

The *Rotnac* (Mensche religious Vocalist) was a short man standing 5'4" tall. He wore a high white square *hapik* on top of his bald head. He chanted some Mensche hymns. His long white robe touched the top of his shoes. The white shawl with Mensche gold writing along one edge hung around his neck and shoulders.

The *Ibbar* (Mensche Religious Leader) stood 6" taller than the *Rotnac* He said some *Mensche* prayers. He wore a long white robe and a white shawl with gold *Mensche* writing along one edge His shawl hung around his neck and shoulders. The *Ibbar* wore a high white square *hapik* on the top of his long curly sandy brown hair. He had long curly sideburns.

My mother was very happy. The *Ibbar* and the *Rotnac* were wearing color coordinated outfits.

At the end of the prayers the Ibbar blessed me and announced my *Mensche* name *"Moyshe born from Michael's sperm."* From that day forward, I was to be known as Moyshe Tushman.

Bubby had the honor of choosing my given name. Six years later, I had a heated argument with her. I insulted *Bubby* when I asked "Who in America would strap a child with the name Moyshe?"

My father had passed out! There was no man in blue to help him off the floor. He missed the "naming."

Mickey and Minerva jumped on top of my father and poured the grape Manischewitz wine on his face.

Bubby slapped my father's face. He woke up and jumped to his feet. My father wasn't embarrassed that he passed out. My mother was embarrassed. My mother screamed at my father because he was a wimp. I was embarrassed for him because he was a wimp.

Fortunately for me, Dr. Max dipped a gauze pad into the grape Manischewitz wine for me to *kinibble.* It took away some of the pain; not all of the pain; only very little of the pain. I believed that the wine did taste very good. "Was I going to grow up to become a drunk? What did I know at the age of eight days old? Did Dr. Max forget something?" He forgot to clean my *schmeckle.* I was looking forward to the cleaning. Barney had told me that it would tickle. It didn't tickle. After the ceremony was over everyone ignored me except *Bubby.* My mother brought me back to the bedroom and placed me in the dark blue crib that had a dark blue linen cover over the mattress.

Barney peeked through the slightly open door of the bedroom with a mischief look in his eyes. He couldn't get into the room fast enough to lick me on the face and squeeze my fingers. *Bubby* was behind Barney. She opened the door further to make sure that I was sleeping. She held Barney by the neck Barney cried when she told him to go back into the living room and play with our twin cousins.

Mickey and Minerva were not jumping on the couch. They were sitting on the red and white checker pattern linoleum floor in the kitchen. They were throwing food at the white painted ceiling. The cream color walls above the pink plastic tiles were covered with eggs. Lox was the food that stuck to the ceiling. Grape *Manischewitz* wine was splashed all over the cream color walls above the pink plastic tiles. There was a lot of food on the floor. My mother was peeved!

Some of the guests were too queasy to watch the circumcision so they watched Howdy Doody and Buffalo Bob on our 14" black and white Motorola television. Several guests went home early. They came only for the food and the grape *Manischewitz* wine.

Bubby vacuumed the living room dark green plush carpet and mopped the dark oak stained hardwood floor in the hallway. She mopped the red and white checker pattern linoleum floor in the kitchen. My mother washed the grape *Manischewitz* wine and food off the kitchen walls. My father sat on his tush and watched them clean until my mother screamed at him. "Michael get off your ass, borrow the neighbor's ladder, climb to the top of the ladder and wash the ceiling." She must have been very upset because she said "ass", not *tush.*

He jumped up off his ass, borrowed the neighbor's ladder, climbed to the top of the ladder and washed the ceiling."

He couldn't move fast enough to satisfy my mother. She kept on screaming until he jumped up off his ass, borrowed the neighbor's ladder, climbed to the top of the ladder and washed the ceiling."

Actually, I learned during the circumcision procedure that I should not have been so excited to look forward to being the "center of attention". To this day; I recall; "IT HURT"! Additionally, now my *schmeckle* looks like a torpedo with a small unlit nightlight bulb on the unattached end. It looked nothing like my uncircumcised *Nudnik* friends.

Bubby helped my mother put the leftover food into the light turquoise color Frigidaire. They hand washed and hand dried all of the plates and silverware. My parents did not own a dishwasher. I had many birthday parties but there were no other special parties in my honor until I became 13 years old, at my *Bar Havztim* in 1957.

Moyshe grew up rapidly after his *Brit Halim. Bubby* couldn't believe how fast the years had passed.

He was becoming very inquisitive about the "birds and the bees,"

CHAPTER IV

THE BIRDS AND THE BEES

*M*oyshe Tushman had one Mission in life: To become a Fountain Pen.

As a pre-teen, Moyshe attended Elementary School 81. He grew up in a *Mensche*–Nudnik neighborhood on the north side of Buffalo.

When Moyshe was a youngster Bubby continued to be an important influence in his life. Grandmother Rifka (née Berlein) Leifver was Moyshe's favorite Bubby. He only had one living maternal grandmother. He never knew Bubby by any other name.

He asked her advice and she offered it willingly. He asked her about life in general and she answered willingly. She had a wonderful, but dry sense of humor. Many of her answers to his questions were interestingly funny.

Moyshe had seen many commercials on television about people in search of their dead ancestors. The people spoke to their dead ancestors whenever they attended a séance. Moyshe was always in search of information about his ancestors. He could not afford a séance so he asked *Bubby* about his ancestors and she answered willingly. Moyshe had other questions that were important to him. He was curious about the "birds and the bees". He believed that the questions had to be answered ASAP.

Moyshe's older brother Barney and his friend Oliver always talked about "sex" and the "birds and the bees". Moyshe was only 8 years old. He did not know what they were talking about.

He asked his parent's about "sex". They ignored him. He asked his parent's about the "birds and the bees". They ignored him. He thought to himself that "sex" and the "birds and bees" must be the same thing because his parents ignored him whenever he asked about either.

After asking a dozen or more times he finally came to the realization that he was never going to get an answer from them. That made him more curious!

Barney was a *puhtz* (dick head) so he wasn't going to tell him. Frankie was a big shot. He thought that he knew everything so he said what he always said, "for me to know and for you to find out". His younger sister Marissa didn't know her ass from a hole in the ground. She certainly couldn't help!

His siblings and friends could not or would not offer an explanation so he had to learn the answer on his own. He looked in his *Mensche-English* Dictionary and his *Bupkis-American* Encyclopedia. He found the definition in the dictionary. The explanation was in medical terms. It was too difficult for him to understand. He found many illustrations in the Encyclopedia. They were in black and white. He could not determine what the illustrations showed because he could only "read" color. He could not look it up on the internet because the Vice President had not discovered the internet yet. Moyshe did not want to embarrass himself so he did not ask his teachers. He was concerned that they would laugh at him or punish him. He didn't realize that his friends were just as ignorant as him until they asked Moyshe the same questions about sex and the "birds and the bees". Moyshe was determined to get the answer so he went to the best source. *Bubby* would have the correct answer.

Moyshe went to the kitchen cupboard to get a cube of sugar. It was Bubby's favorite sweetener. She used it when she drank her tea. She poured the tea from her tea cup into a saucer to cool it. Then she put the sugar cube in her mouth between her teeth. As she sipped the tea, she sucked on the sugar cube. Her two front upper and two front lower teeth were missing so the sugar cube fit in between her teeth perfectly.

Moyshe approached her with the sugar cube in his left hand. He offered Bubby the sugar cube. His left arm was stretched out too far; he tripped and he almost poked her right eye out of the socket. He apologized profusely as he ran to the kitchen refrigerator to get *Bubby* a slice of cold kosher salami to cover her black and blue swelling eye. He knew that a steak would work better. However his parents never bought steak because it was too expensive.

Moyshe sat on *Bubby's* lap and cuddled. He placed his *keppelah* (head) snugly on her squishy oblong breasts. He put his arms around her thick waist. She especially enjoyed the "cuddling". *Bubby* knew that she was being "played". It didn't matter because she enjoyed being "played" by Moyshe.

He was confident that he could ask her about "sex" and the "birds and the bees" because she would not laugh at him. Moyshe posed the question! "What is sex and what is the story about the "birds and the bees?"

Bubby gave it much thought before she answered him. He was only 8 years old and in 3rd grade at Elementary School 81. She did not want Moyshe's parents Michael and Michelle to get upset with her answer.

She told him that "sex" and the "birds and bees" were the same thing. I was correct. They were the same thing. She continued with the explanation. It was very special. Sex is when a man and a woman were both completely naked. They leaned their heads toward each other. The man's lips would press lightly against the woman's lips and they would stand two feet apart. There were no pictures in the encyclopedia that were similar. Bubby was smarter than anyone he knew so she was certainly smarter than the illustrators that drew pictures in the encyclopedia. They must not have known how to draw pictures of sex or they probably did not know what it meant. He saw birds and bees flying everywhere. He queried "How could the "birds and the bees" be the same as sex? Although they never wore clothes, they never flied close enough to each other to press their lips together." After *Bubby* gave Moyshe the explanation he told her that he wanted to practice sex. She told him that it was okay to practice sex but he had to practice with his clothes on until he was married. It was okay to practice sex with his clothes off only if he was alone. Moyshe was confused. He did not understand; clothes on or clothes off?

Although Moyshe did not understand, he was satisfied with *Bubby's* explanation! <u>*Bubby*</u> knew that Michael and Michelle would be satisfied with her response to Moyshe's question.

Now that he knew the answer, Moyshe decided that his *Mission in Life* would be to have sex. He told *Bubby* his *Mission in Life* because he trusted her not to tell his parents.

Moyshe's *Mission in Life* was to have as much sex as possible with his clothes off and not to have sex alone. He knew that it took two lips to have sex. Eventually, he would realize that he was going to be very disappointed many times in life.

No matter what he did and no matter where he went Moyshe always had his *Mission* in Life on his mind. He thought about it so often that he had to consult a neurologist to help him clear his head of terrible migraine headaches. When that didn't work he consulted a psychologist to get sex completely out of his mind. That didn't work. He asked *Bubby* what to do to get sex and the "Birds and the Bees" out of his mind.

Bubby told him that he may never get sex out of his mind because many of his ancestors always had sex and the"Birds and the Bees" on their minds. The desire to have sex was in their DNA. It was in their *genes*. Moyshe didn't know the meaning *of DNA* and he thought it was weird that she said birds and bees were in their jeans. He didn't know how to spell *genes,* let alone what it meant. He wondered if his ancestors ever got stung inside their jeans. If they did, their *schmeckle* (penis) would probably swell. Maybe it wasn't such a bad thing to get stung. Moyshe was positive that his ancestors must have spent a lot of money on neurologists, psychologists and aspirins. They probably spent as much as his parents spent to try to cure him of his neuroses.

Moyshe's favorite magazines were *Playboy* and *Mad*. He examined every picture on every page in search of the true answer to sex.

Moyshe did not want his parents to know that he owned those magazines. He could not hide the magazines in his own dresser drawer. He hid them under the boxer shorts in Barney's dresser drawer. If His mother found the magazines, Barney's *tush* would be on the line. It would have been funny for Moyshe to see Barney's tu*sh hanging* on the clothes line. His *tush* would not be on the line.

Moyshe perused the magazines at night under his favorite cowboy blanket *Hopalong Cassidy and Silver*. His minuscule *Dick Tracy* flashlight shined bright enough to accentuate the Playboy Bunnies' curvaceous large breasts and small *tushies*. The colorful pictures were easy to "read" on the glossy pages.

Moyshe couldn't understand why the pages were sometimes wet and sticky. The pictures were faded after Barney read the *Playboy Magazine*. He asked *Bubby*. She said "*gay schlafen* (go to sleep). I'll tell you in the morning." The next morning Moyshe awoke early to get the answer. *Bubby* told him that the magazine was wet because it fell in to the toilet.

Alfred E. Newman was *Mad Magazine's* fictitious mascot. Newman's face was distinguished by large ears, a missing front tooth and one eye lower than the other. His eyebrows were high above his eyes. Newman was Moyshe's hero. Moyshe didn't realize that he was not going to learn about sex from *Mad Magazine* because he didn't know that Alfred E. Newman was not married and he was too young to know anything about sex.

Moyshe didn't realize that he was not going to learn about sex from *Playboy Magazine* because he only gazed at the girls' *breasts* and *tushies* for hours at a time. He never read the articles. There was not one picture of men and women having sex. Many pictures showed them completely naked, lying next to each other with their bodies and lips touching. However, that couldn't be sex because none of the pictures showed them standing up, two feet apart from each other. They were always lying down. Sometimes they were on top of each other but they were never standing up

Moyshe showed the pictures to *Bubby*. She told him that the person on top was the winner of the wrestling match. Sometimes the woman won. Most times the man won. Moyshe asked if it was ever an even match when no one lost or won. *Bubby* said that there were many even matches. Nobody lost! Everybody won!

MOYSHE'S MATERNAL GRANDMOTHER BUBBY RIFKA

CHAPTER I

BUBBY RIFKA HER LIFE

Bubby's husband Baytsim had abandoned her. None of her children lived in Buffalo except Michelle.

Bubby lived alone until she moved into her son-in-law Michael and daughter Michelle's home during Moyshe's pre-teen years.

Bubby was a kind, soft-spoken woman. She was born in America. She was 5'1" tall. She was *zaftig* (fully rounded figure) and she had an oval face with a small wart on the tip of her bulbous nose. *Bubby* seldom went outside during the day so she never had a sun tan. Her skin tone was very light and her eyes were a light gray color. Moyshe did not know the length of Bubby's salt and pepper color hair. She always wore it pulled back with a bun on top of her head. The bun was held together by a wide dark red rubber band. She always wore wide dark red rubber bands around her wrist as extras just in case the rubber band in her hair broke or was lost.

Many of *Bubby's* stories were humorous, if you like dry humor. Many of her stories were not humorous. Many of *Bubby's* answers to Moyshe's questions were humorous. Many of the answers to Moyshe's questions were not humorous. She had to have a sense of humor in order to tell Moyshe some of her sad stories. She experienced many hardships. *Bubby* teased Moyshe quite often. She teased him whenever she had the opportunity.

He was thankful that *Bubby* told him many stories of his ancestors. He believed that he inherited many of their traits. That gave him a good sense of understanding about his own behavior and beliefs. Moyshe believed that he certainly had inherited the "birds and the bees" in his jeans because his ancestors had the "birds" and the bees" in their jeans. Moyshe's ancestors observed *Mensche* religion. He observed *Mensche* religion as did his ancestors.

Bubby's parents spoke *gantz gut* (very good) *Mensche*, the primary language in Bupkis. Moyshe's paternal and maternal Great Grandparents learned English when they arrived in America. It was not easy for them to learn English because of their heavy Mensche accent. It was difficult for them to pronounce the English words so no one knew if they were actually speaking the English language. They spoke *farpotshket* (broken) English. *Bubby* spoke *gut* English and *gantz gut Mensche*.

She told Moyshe that he would understand why his *Mission in Life* to become a "Fountain Pen" was so important if he knew more about his ancestors. Several of his Grandfathers always had sex on their minds. It was in their genes. They had the same *Mission in Life* as *Moyshe's Mission* in *Life*.

Whenever *Bubby* told Moyshe stories about her own family, he could see tears well up in her eyes. She recalled many of the hardships in her life as she told her stories. *Bubby* experienced the deaths of her parents and several siblings. Her youngest brother Benjamin suffered a disability. Her father Ayzak was unfaithful to *Bubby's* mother Bella. Bu*bby's* husband *Baytsim* was unfaithful to her.

Bubby's father Ayzak was born in Misktown, the capital of Suraleb.

Ayzak was handsome. He was 5'5" tall. He had thick dark brown hair neatly combed at all times. He had bushy dark brown eyebrows that were high above his brown eyes. To compensate for his short height, Ayzak lifted weights, jogged and exercised quite often to stay fit and trim.

Ayzak migrated from Bupkis, Europe to America when he was twenty-one years old. He settled in Hartford, Connecticut. His brother Julius lived in Hartford. Julius introduced him to Bella. Julius remained in Hartford Ayzak and Bella said their vows. They were married in Hartford. They moved to Buffalo, New York. Their first child *Bubby* was born in Buffalo.

According to Bubby, Ayzak was a good father but not a good husband. Many nights he came home drunk from the local taverns of Buffalo. He was a women chaser. He paid to have sex with prostitutes before he married Bella. Ayzak continued to pay to have sex with them after he married Bella. He didn't pay to have sex with Bella.

Ayzak only came home late at night to have sex with Bella in order to make babies. It didn't matter to him that she was sleeping. Most of the time, he didn't have to wake her to have sex. It took less than three minutes. He enjoyed sex so much that he and Bella had nine children. She didn't enjoy sex. Two children died directly after child birth. Ayzak kept Bella barefoot and pregnant during most of their married life.

Ayzak was a tailor by trade. He was a very good tailor. He earned a sufficient income to support his family, drink Vodka and pay for his prostitutes.

He enjoyed playing with his children. He spent a lot of time with them every Saturday and Sunday. Saturday was the *Sabbath* (Day of Rest) so he didn't work. According to *Mensche* religion you could not drive or work on the *Sabbath,* the seventh day of the week. Mensche people believed that the *Supreme Being* created the world in six days and rested on the seventh day, the *Sabbath.* On Sunday Ayzak drove the children to Temple for their Mensche lessons. After Temple they went to the *International House of Kishka* to eat their favorite lunch. It consisted of *kishka,* bacon, eggs and orange juice. Bella stayed home because she was tired from *shtooping* so often. She played with the children and did house work Monday through Friday. She prayed all day Saturday that Ayzak would not shtoop her every evening. Sunday was her day to play canasta with her friends. During Bella's eleven pregnancies she was more than tired. She was exhausted from *shtooping* Ayzak even though it never lasted more than three minutes each time. She dreaded Ayzak's *schmeckle*. Ayzak told his siblings and friends that he was a women chaser because he had the "birds and the bees" in his genes. He loved *shtooping*.

Ayzak won a silver medal for shtooping. His brother Julius won the gold medal. It was a popular event in the Bupkis Olympics. Every man participated. There were no Buffalo Olympics. Although Ayzak had many indiscretions Bella must have loved him very much. Why else would she suffer through eleven pregnancies?

Bubby was the oldest child. She had seven sisters and one brother. Ayzak was desperate to have a son. He stopped pushing fast when he shtooped Bella. He was told that the baby's *schmeckle* would not fall off if he pushed slowly.

It worked. Their son Benjamin was born after Bella's tenth pregnancy. After Benjamin was born Ayzak started to push faster.

Bella took several walks on the green grass in the nearby park after Benjamin was born.

It was a bitter sweet day when Benjamin was born. They finally had a son. Bella was always barefoot when she took those walks. There were many deer romping in the park. She attracted ticks and she came down with Lyme disease. The disease was very painful and dangerous. Lyme disease and the pregnancies drained her energy. Her immune system reached an all time low. Bella was bed ridden for the rest of her life. Ayzak didn't care that she was bed ridden.

She was very ill. Ayzak went out more often to be with his prostitutes. He did not concern himself with Bella's health. Ayzak did not help Bella. He refused to vacuum the carpet. He refused to dust the furniture. He refused to cook He refused to wash and dry the dishes. He was most adamant that he would not change or wash the diapers.

Bubby's siblings were too selfish, too young or too ill to help with the chores. She became responsible for all household chores and the care of her father and siblings.

Bubby's sister Sheila was one year younger than her. She was very selfish so she didn't help with the chores and she got away with it because she was never at home. According to *Bubby,* Sheila was one of the prettiest girls in the neighborhood. Many boys dated Sheila until she turned seventeen years old. She had become arrogant about her beauty compared to the other girls. She took advantage of her beauty. She teased the other girls and convinced the boys that those girls were too *mieskeit* (ugly) to date.

Eventually, the boys tired of Sheila's selfish, arrogant attitude so they stopped dating her.

Desperate to recapture the attention of the boys, Sheila became a *shlooche* (slut) .She put out for any boy that wore pants, Even Rufus, the *Nudnik* (non -Mensche boy) became tired of her arrogance. Sheila never married.

Sally *was mieskeit.* She was one year younger than Sheila. The boys teased her and referred to her as *mieskeit* Sally. She was very insecure because she was one of the *mieskeit* girls that Sheila talked about. The boys thought that Sally would be easy to *shtoop* because she would be desperate to date them. They were wrong! Sally thought that she could hold out from shtooping because the boys that didn't want to date Sheila would ask her for a date. She was wrong!

Sally never had a date. She became depressed and ran away from home; never to be found.

Sandra was very intelligent. She graduated from high school. She was the first in her family to do so! Her grades were so good that she was accepted to *Bupkis at Buffalo Sewing Trade College.* Sandra never graduated because she had two problems.

She did not have enough money to pay tuition to complete her education and very few people needed a seamstress. People in the neighborhood were very poor. They did their own sewing. Sandra did have a few small jobs. She had to borrow money from Ayzak to pay for thread for the few small jobs.

Men did not pursue Sandra because she constantly complained about money and the loan that she had borrowed from Ayzak. The men were afraid that they would have to make the loan payments. They did not know that Ayzak was a good father and that he did not press Sandra to pay the $1.75 per month to repay the $35 loan. Sandra was not able to repay Ayzak. She stayed at home. *Bubby* took care of her.

Stella and Selma, the twins loved Ayzak very much because he played with them every Saturday and Sunday. They couldn't afford to leave home. Sephora was too young to wander the streets. *Bubby* wouldn't let her leave home.

Sara, the youngest of the sisters had an unfortunate accident when she was six years old. She was sitting on an old truck tire that was hanging from a rope attached to an oak tree in their backyard. It was a home-made swing.

Sarah ate a banana every time that she was swinging on the tire. One Saturday afternoon that Sara was swinging on the tire a sudden snow storm unexpectedly started. The weatherman had predicted that it would be a clear sunny day. He was wrong. Sarah was eating a hard, green banana. The tire became slippery from the snow. She fell off the swing and landed onto her face. The banana jammed into her throat. She choked to death. *Bubby* sat *Shiva* for five days. *Shiva* is a mourning period in the *Mensche* Religion. A person that was sitting *Shiva* did not go out of the house. *Bubby* chanted *Mensche* prayers to honor her deceased sister. *Bubby* was very sad. However, she continued to do the household chores.

Bubby adored her little brother Benjamin. He was tiny and frail. She was very protective of him. Benjamin became ill and could not walk without assistance so *Bubby* took long walks while pushing his stroller.

Bubby's mother Bella became very depressed from all of her misfortune. She died at a young age. She was 41 years old.

On a cold evening in February, *Bubby's* father Ayzak was in the local tavern drinking Vodka. At 7:00 PM a heavy winter storm left a four inches blanket of snow on the ground. The temperature became warmer by 9:00 PM. The snow became rain. The rain caused the snow to become slush. The temperature became cold again by 10:00 PM. The slush became ice. The ice solidified on the sidewalk In front of the tavern.

Ayzak left the tavern at 11:00 PM. He was inebriated. It was very dark. Ayzak couldn't see beyond his nose. He was unsteady on his feet. He slipped on a patch of ice.

Ayzak fell down and broke his crown. He died instantly! *Bubby* was sad. She sat *Shiva* for five days. She had to work to earn money to put food on the table.

Moyshe never met his maternal Grandfather. He was *Bubby's* husband. His name was Baytsim Leifver. He was born in Boston, Massachusetts. *Baytsim* moved to New York City before he joined the Navy in October, 1913. He was honorably discharged in April, 1915 for medical reasons. He had warts on the bottom of his feet. He could not wear flippers for swimming. His eyes became blood shot whenever he dove underwater. He could not see through the face mask if he was underwater for more than 12 seconds.

Baytsim went on vacation to Buffalo, New York. His brother Ronald lived in Buffalo. He introduced Baytsim to *Bubby*.

Bubby said that *Baytsim* was a good looking man. He stood tall at 5'11". He had a medium frame body. His perfectly combed wavy dark brown hair was parted on the left side. *Baytsim's* bushy brown eyebrows formed a semi-circle above his light blue left eye and light green right eye.

Baytsim liked Buffalo very much. He moved to Buffalo permanently in February, 1916. He courted *Bubby* for several months before they were married. They were married in December, 1916. He treated her like a princess during the courtship.

Bubby's siblings moved in to Baytsim and her home so that she could take care of them. Baytsim and *Bubby*, with all of her siblings lived in a four bedroom apartment building in downtown Buffalo.

Baytsim was the love of Bubby's life at that time. He agreed to allow *Bubby's* siblings to live in their apartment. He hired a full time female companion to help *Bubby* do the house work and take care of her siblings. Some people questioned his real intentions to hire a female companion that was thirteen years younger than *Bubby*. She was probably a *shlooche*.

Bubby did not have a driver's license. Baytsim drove her everywhere.

They went on several picnics to different orchards in Orchard, New York. They picked apples, oranges and grapes in the apples oranges and grapes orchards. *Bubby* washed the fruit at home and inspected them to pull out the worms.

They took many Sunday drives along the Lewiston escarpment and Niagara River. Once a month they drove to Niagara Falls, New York to view the colorful lights that shined on the waterfalls from 10:00 PM to 11:30 PM every Friday. *Bubby* told Moyshe that they stopped at a small confectionery store at the corner of Niagara Street and Third Avenue in Niagara Falls. They bought caramel coated popcorn. The caramel was sticky. The popcorn stuck together because of the sticky caramel. The store owner made the sticky popcorn in the shape of a small "barrel". *Bubby* bought two "barrels" to share with her siblings.

Bubby showed Moyshe a black and white photo of her and Baytsim going over the waterfalls in a small wood canoe. She wore a pretty light blue dress that appeared to be light gray in the black and white photo. Moyshe believed that *Bubby* and Baytsim actually did go over the waterfalls. She finally told Moyshe that the photo was not real when he became nine years old.

Bubby told him that Baytsim, her siblings and she went swimming at Bay Beach in the Village of Crystal Beach on warm summer days. They traveled in Ayzak's 1917 black Ford Touring Automobile. A few of the children sat on the floor in the back.

On several Saturday nights she wore her light blue dress to dance at the Crystal Palace located in the Crystal Beach Amusement Park.

On some weekends they enjoyed picnics in Ellicott Creek Park. Baytsim rented a canoe for himself. *Bubby* and her siblings watched him paddle the canoe up and down the creek. He waived to all of the ladies that stood along the shoreline. They waived back.

Baytsim and Bubby celebrated their anniversaries at the *Town Casino* or *Laube's* Restaurant in downtown Buffalo. The *Town Casino* was a nightclub that featured dinner and entertainment. A variety of entertainers sang, told jokes and tap danced for the audiences.

Baytsim and *Bubby*, not to be out done by Bubby's parents, had nine children. Isabella and Rochelle volunteered at the soup kitchen. During the winter they brought food home. Michelle and Molly delivered newspapers to earn money. Jacob and Harold enlisted in the army during WWII. Robert, Ira and Leonard were too young to enlist. They stayed home and took care of the gold fish and tadpoles.

Baytsim learned to be a tailor from his father-in-law Ayzak to support his family. Baytsim was not a good tailor. He earned very little money. He was not a good husband. He was not a good father. He was not a responsible person. He did not support his large family because he could not earn enough money. He could not tolerate the constant crying of the younger children.

Baytsim became a chip off his father-in-law's old block. He drank Vodka straight from the bottle He became inebriated quite often in the small local taverns in Buffalo. He did not physically or verbally abuse *Bubby* or the children but he did avoid being near them.

Bubby said that Baytsim was very handsome so he did not have any trouble attracting women. She was aware of his shenanigans but she loved him very much so she did not do anything about his indiscretions.

Baytsim could not afford to pay prostitutes. He did enjoy the companionship of many women at least twice a week. He *shtooped* many women. They did not mind cheating on their husbands. Their husbands were in Europe assisting the cleanup of the war torn countries from the aftermath of WWI. They cheated on their wives so the women cheated on their husbands. The men were busy *shtooping* Germland Frauleins and Francland Mademoiselles when they were not shoveling *drek* (crap) off the streets.

Baytsim stayed out late most of the time. He did come home early enough on weekends to *shtoop Bubby*. He refused to put on a condom, get a vasectomy or get castrated. She refused to get her tubes tied or swallow a contraceptive pill. It was against Mensche beliefs. He impregnated her nine times and kept her barefoot all of the time. Baytsim would not allow *Bubby* to buy shoes. It was not because he was mean. It was because he couldn't afford them. He spent most of his money at the *Town Casino* or drinking *Vodka* in the local Buffalo Bars.

Bubby owned a pair of worn out slippers for indoors and outdoors. The children wore shoes that were handed down to them by their older cousins. *Bubby* did not chase Baytsim when he stormed out of the house because she was afraid of cutting the bottom of her feet or stubbing her toes on the large stones atop the sidewalks. She was also afraid that she would get Lyme disease.

Baytsim ignored the needs of *Bubby* and their children. The small amount of money that he had in his pocket was spent on Vodka and gambling.

He did drive her to wherever she wanted to go if it was for his benefit. His driver's license was suspended. He was penalized three times for DWI. *Bubby* continually tried to obtain a driver's license. She never had a driver's license because she failed the test eleven times. That's what happened. She never learned how to drive because Baytsim wouldn't teach her. He couldn't afford to pay for driving lessons. The children were too young to drive.

After one year Baytsim had his driver's license returned to him. One week later, he drove through a stop sign. There was an open bottle of *Vodka* on his lap when a policeman stopped him. The policeman issued him a ticket.

Baptism's driver's license was not suspended. It was revoked.

Bubby had to ride a three wheel bicycle when Baytsim's driver's license was revoked. There was a large basket in the back of the bicycle for *Bubby* to carry the groceries. Baytsim refused to ride the bicycle. He would have been too embarrassed.

Bubby washed and ironed her neighbors' clothes so that she could have enough money to put food on the table.

When *Bubby* told Baytsim stories about the way her father Ayzak treated her mother Bella, Baytsim became jealous of his father-in-law. Although his father-in-law was dead, Baytsim was still jealous of him. It became worse. He began to follow the footsteps of his father-in-law. *Bubby* with tears in her eyes took a deep sigh as she reminisced about her own life as a young woman. She recalled that Baytsim was a wonderful man before they were married. That changed after they were married.

The evening of their 20th anniversary *B*aytsim went to the downtown Buffalo Burlesque. It was a strip club. He made sure that he came home late enough so that *Bubby* would be sound asleep. He packed his bags and abandoned *Bubby* and their children. Baytsim's Friend Stash Slalom drove him to Tampa, Florida. Baytsim was never to be seen again by his family.

Moyshe's mother Michelle was Baytsim and *Bubby's* fifth child. Although *Bubby* forgave Baytsim for abandoning the family, Michelle never forgave him. The other children forgave him. Baytsim never re-married. He lived with a woman in Tampa. Her name was Nellie. Michelle never met Nellie. She nicknamed Nellie, Nafka (whore).

Baytsim and Nafka had a daughter. Her name was Patsy. Michelle never met Patsy. She nicknamed her *Schnook*. She supported Nellie and Baytsim. Schnook was a pre-school teacher's assistant. Every penny that she earned was spent on Baytsim and Nafka.

Baytsim died in 1939. To everyone's surprise, he had a will. He bequeathed his "fortunes" as follows. Nafka and Schnook received $25,000 each. *Bubby* and each of the children received $75 each. Michelle received nothing.

Moyshe was positive that his maternal Great Grandfather Ayzak and Grandfather Baytsim had "birds and bees" in their jeans. Moyshe was positive that he inherited the "Birds and Bees" from them.

Bubby did not know very much about her Grandfather Platzim, Great Grandfather Leyba or any of her other ancestors.

She did not tell Moyshe any other stories about her family. He believed that there were probably many other stories about her family but they must have been too painful to share with him. If she wouldn't share those stories with Moyshe, she certainly would not share them with anyone else.

Bubby enjoyed telling stories about other families to Moyshe. He enjoyed listening. *Bubby* insisted that she was not a *Yenta* (Busy body) even though only 2% of the stories were about her own family, 85% of the stories were about Moyshe's paternal ancestors and 13% of the stories were about the neighbors. According to Bubby the stories had to be true because her mother and grandmother had told them to her. They insisted that the stories were true.

It was her pleasure to tell stories to Moyshe. He was *Bubby's* second grandchild. She told him that he was her favorite grandchild because he listened attentively to her stories. The other grandchildren ignored her. Moyshe was not sure which stories were exaggerations.

Bubby spoke English when she told the stories to him. However, she spoke Mensche when she did not want Moyshe to understand the foul language that she spoke quite often.

According to *Bubby,* she never smoked cigarettes, cigars or pipes and she never drank alcohol. She only used *schnapps* to put on her bulbous nose to breathe better. Moyshe did see her take a nip or two, once in awhile when she thought that no one was looking. He never saw her smoke cigarettes or cigars. He did see her smoke a peace pipe one time. It was after she had a heated argument with her son-in-law Michael. Moyshe did not understand why they put their pointer finger over their lips, giggled and kept smoking the peace pipe until Moyshe's mother Michelle came into the room. He always wondered what was in the pipe. It didn't smell like tobacco!

Bubby did not think that Moyshe understood Mensche. She swore often. He bought a Mensche-English dictionary so that he could translate the Mensche swear words. *Bubby* did not know that he owned the dictionary. He had to hold back from laughing when she swore.

Many times Moyshe walked around the neighborhood shouting profanities in Mensche. He could not understand why the neighbors chuckled. He did not realize that most adults in the neighborhood were first or second generation American *Mensche*. They understood Mensche language. His parents did not chuckle!

Moyshe stopped swearing when he developed a horrible taste in his mouth. His parents constantly washed his mouth with soap and water to teach him a lesson not to swear. The lesson was well learned. Eventually the taste disappeared. One good thing came from his swearing. He had the cleanest mouth in the neighborhood.

Moyshe's paternal and maternal grandparents knew each other. The four of them met when they lived in the same neighborhood on the west side of Buffalo.

They lived on Prospect Avenue under the Peace Bridge. They were not trolls. They did not live directly under the bridge. Prospect Avenue passed under the bridge.

The Tushman family shared many stories about Moyshe's paternal ancestors. *Bubby* had plenty of material to tell Moyshe.

MOYSHE'S PATERNAL ANCESTORS

CHAPTER I

ZITSONTUSH FAMILY

Moyshe's ancestors lived in Bupkis, Europe. They observed *Mensche* Religion. *Mensche* people were constantly being persecuted by Nudniks, non believers.

The Tushman family name was Zitsontush until Herman Zitsontush changed it to Tushman when he moved to America in 1893.

Bubby told her version of the story about *Adam & Eva* because she insisted that they were Moyshe's ancestors.

CHAPTER II

ADAM & EVA ZITSONTUSH

The story of "Adam and Eva" is essential to the *Mensche* religion. The first chapter of the *Mensche Tovrah* (History Book) advocates the belief that Adam and Eva lived in a Secret Garden on *Diamond Island* in the middle of Lake Superior in Canada. Adam lived on the east side of the Secret Garden. Eva lived on the west side.

Adam exercised every day. He climbed the tall sour grape vines on the island. He was very thin because he exercised every day and he had only one rib. He had curly black hair that was shoulder length. His long curly sideburns grew to the front of his face forming an unkempt mustache and beard. Adam's hairy chest, legs, arms and back kept him warm on cold, rainy days. Eva had a curvaceous figure. Her kumquat shaped breasts, and slender waist accentuated her watermelon size *tush*. There was not any hair salon on the island so it was evident that her blonde hair was natural. It was not dyed blonde.

The island was owned by *King Goodt N. Badt*, herein after known as "*The King*". He was a short man standing at 5'3". His thick fire engine red beard grew down to his Buddha size belly. The hot rays of the yellow-orange sun bounced off his tanned bald head. He had a daughter named *Princess Sweet N. Sour* (herein after known as *"The Princess"*). The Princess looked like her father. She had a Buddha size belly and bald head. Her cantaloupe size breasts rested on her belly. She was born out of wedlock.

The King was born in the country of Suraleb in Europe. He had a harem of eight women. After all is said, he was the king. It was good to be king!

One night in the middle of summer, *The King* hosted a ball at his gigantic yellow stone castle. The castle was surrounded by a moat of deep water. A beautiful young maiden named *"Emerald"* approached and asked him to dance with her. *The King* accepted. He knew how the night would end. He sent his harem of eight women to romp in the *Royal Guest Quarters* while he danced with the young maiden *Emerald.* His harem of eight women drank an abundant amount of wine and romped on the King Size Bed until they tired and fell asleep in the heat of the summer night.

The King ordered the *Royal Philharmonic Orchestra* to play slow music. He held *Emerald* close to his chest as they danced the *Suraleb Waltz.* He whispered in to her ear "come to my Royal Bedroom and I will worship you and name the land in the middle of the English Channel *Emerald Island.* She questioned *The King;* "How can we go to the *Royal Bedroom* with your eight women romping?"

The King told her that his harem of eight women romped and slept in only two quarters of the *Royal Bedroom.* He and Emerald would retire to the other two quarters. She was convinced that *The King* was a *"wise man".* Four Royal Quarters totaled one Royal Bedroom.

Nine months later, Emerald gave birth *to Princess Sweet N. Sour.*

The King tired of *Emerald* and his harem of eight women so he and his daughter *Princess Sweet N. Sour* hopped on to the ship *Destination* that was headed to America. *Emerald* hired a good attorney to force *The King* to pay alimony even though they never married. The attorney negotiated a favorable contract for Emerald.

Emerald kept the island and began to live with the attorney.

They did not anticipate the high cost to maintain the island. They went bankrupt. *The King* sent a proxy to bid on the bankrupt island. He was the highest bidder. He bought the island out of bankruptcy at a cost $75. He had originally inherited the island from his father *King* Robby. No one else could afford to bid.

The King and *The Princess* boarded the ship that was docked on the west side of Emerald Island.

Heavy storms caused high waves in the Atlantic Ocean to force the ship to sail off course. Instead of sailing toward the intended destination T*he Fountain of Youth* in Florida the ship headed north to the St. Lawrence Seaway which passed through Lake Ontario, Lake Erie, Lake Huron, and Lake Michigan. The journey ended at Lake Superior on the Canadian side of the lake. *The King* bought a beautiful island with a *Secret Garden* where he and his bastard daughter would live. The *King* never found the *Fountain of Youth*. It was never discovered even though for several years the Spanish explorer *Ponce on Leo* searched for it until he died of old age.

The King Goodt N. Badt told *The Princess Sweet N. Sour* to plant two vines in the *Secret Garden*. He didn't want to get his hands dirty. One vine had delicious red grapes and the other vine had sour green grapes. *The King* and *The Princess* were the only people allowed to eat the delicious red grapes. The red grapes were *Forbidden Fruits* so everyone else was not allowed to eat them. *The King* and *The Princess* had double personalities. *The King* was good and evil. The Princess was sweet and sour. *The Princess* had no friends except Eva. They were BFF (Best Friends Forever). They shared their deepest secrets. Eva told the Princess that Adam wanted to *shtoop (screw)* Eva so that they could have a child. Every person on earth *shtooped* and every baby on earth were born out of wedlock.

Eva wanted to set a precedent. She insisted that Adam marry her before she would allow him to *shtoop* her. Adam agreed to it only if Eva would make all of the arrangements for the wedding. He didn't want to make any decisions. *The Princess* helped Eva with the plans. She suggested that Adam and Eva have the ceremony in the middle of the Secret Garden. Her father owned the island so he owned the Secret Garden. She asked The *King* to officiate at the ceremony. They did not have to hire a florist because the beautiful flowers in the Secret Garden had already been blooming for hundreds of years. The flowers had blossomed and they were ready for picking.

Marvin the evil Magician did not approve of the wedding because he did not want Adam and Eva to set a precedent about the need to marry before a couple could *shtoop* to give birth to a child. He was very vocal about his disapproval. As punishment for disrespecting his wishes, *The King* insisted that Marvin attend the wedding. Marvin would be the only witness to the ceremony.

The Princess decided to give Adam and Eva the perfect gift. All of *the King's* horses pulled carts full of wood for all of *The King's* men to build a small cottage for Adam and Eva to live in the middle of the Secret Garden.

The wedding provided the basis for the *Mensche* belief that humanity is in essence a single family and everyone descended from a single pair of original ancestors.

The King allowed Adam and Eva to live in the cottage in the middle of the Secret Garden as long as they adhered to his rules. Adam and Eva would be punished if they did not obey his rules. There were two paths that started in the middle of the Secret Garden. One path led to the *Forbidden Red Grapes* of which Adam and Eva were prohibited from eating. The other path led to the vines of sour green grapes of which Adam and Eva were allowed to eat.

Adam was told that he did not have to pay rent. He only had to water the grass, the flowers and the red and green grape vines

The right path led to the vines full of sour green grapes and the wrong path led to the *Forbidden vines* of delicious red grapes.

Every day Adam walked the right path to gather sour green grapes for Eva and him to eat.

One day Marvin the evil Magician decided to get even with Adam and Eva for setting the precedent about *shtooping*. On a day that Adam was away from the cottage for a walk on the right path, Marvin was walking on the wrong path. He stole some red grapes from the *Forbidden Vines*. He ran quickly toward the cottage.

Marvin knocked on the door thirteen times. Eva opened the door and invited Marvin to come into the cottage. They were having an affair. Eva trusted Marvin not to say a word to Adam. Marvin was also having an affair with *The Princess*. He found out that Eva was having an affair with *The King*. Marvin was upset with Eva. To get even with her he tricked Eva to take a bite out of the delicious red grape. He told her that no harm would come to her because his magic powers would keep harm away.

Eva took a bite and nothing bad happened. When Adam returned to home that day Marvin ran out of the back door. He avoided getting caught by Adam with his pants down. Eva told Adam to take a bite from a delicious red grape. She told him that it was sweet, not sour like the green grapes. She told him that Marvin had told her that no harm would come to them. Adam refused to bite into the *Forbidden Fruit* until Eva threatened him. "Take a bite or I will never let you shtoop me again". It took exactly 33 seconds for Adam to eat the *Forbidden Fruit.* That provided much of the scriptural basis for the doctrines of the fall of man and original Sin, important beliefs in *Mensche* Religion.

Marvin was a vindictive magician. He squealed on them. He told *The King* that Adam and Eva ate the *Forbidden Fruit*.

The King rewarded Marvin for telling him about Adam and Eva's disobedience. He gave Marvin the authority to use his magic to punish Adam and Eva.

Marvin put a curse on them and their pet *Serpent.* The Serpent's curse was that it would be feared by all human beings. The serpent would lose its hands and feet. The serpent could no longer be allowed to be Adam and Eva's pet. It would have to slither along the ground to move from one place to another.

Adam and Eva's curse was that they could no longer live in the cottage in the *Secret Garden* and they were banished from the Secret Garden. Additionally, they were stripped of their clothing and they could only wear fig leafs to cover their private parts. The fig leafs would only cover Adam's *schmeckle* and Eva's *coochie* and kinipples.

Their *tushies* would get frost bite from the snow on the ground during the winter and they would get dirty during the fall and spring from sitting in the mud. They were only allowed to swim in Lake Superior during the summer to clean their tushies.

The Serpent slowly slithered toward Adam and Eva on the last day of spring. It was only able to look up from the ground. Adam and Eva's tushies were exposed. Eva's *tush* was smooth and round but it was extremely huge. That was her punishment. Adam's tush had *zits* (pimples) on it. That was his punishment.

The Serpent stared at Adam's *tush* and gave him sad news. *The King* told the Serpent that it would be known as *Snake* and Adam's family name would be *Zitsontush (Pimples on his ass)*

There were four seasons on Diamond Island. There was bird watching during autumn, skiing during the winter, horseback riding during the spring and swimming during the summer.

Satan the Devil wanted to buy the island. He was going to turn the island into an all seasons resort area. *The King* sold the island *to Satan the Devil* for $23.50 which was 50 cents less than the Dutch paid to the American Indians for Manhattan Island. *The Agreement* was that *Satan* would not eat the *Forbidden Fruit. Satan* accepted the *Agreement.*

The President of *Paradise* Cruise Line Company wanted to make a deal with *the Devil.* He owned private islands in the warm climate of the Caribbean but he did not own any islands with four seasons. He needed the island all year round for his vacationing customers. *Satan* honored his *Agreement* with *The King.* He insisted that there would be no land excursions to the Secret Garden so no one would be able to *nosh* (snack) on *the Forbidden Fruit.*

The President of the Cruise Line agreed to the terms and conditions. Actually, the *Devil* wanted to keep the delicious red grapes for himself. He didn't care about the sour green grapes. *Satan* received $1,550,000 from the sale. *The Devil broke the Agreement* he saw the opportunity to make a large profit from selling products to the vacationers. He sold red grapes at a fruit stand that he set up at the entrance to the ship and the exit off the island. *The King* found out about the Fruit Stand. He hired a lawyer to get an injunction against T*he Devil.* To *The King's* dismay he was told by his lawyer that the Judge had made a deal with *The Devil.* The Judge received 2% of the revenue from the sales at the Fruit Stand. The Judge would not allow an injunction. *The Devil* continued to sell the red grapes.

Adam and Eva Zitsontush had many children. Their oldest son was Noah Zitsontush.

NOAH ZITSONTUSH
MOYSHE'S 12ᵀᴴ GRANDFATHER

I t rained for forty days and forty nights. Noah's friend George Washingsome would not help Noah chop down the *Forbidden Grape Vines* for Noah to use the wood of the vines to build an ark. George explained that he only chopped down cherry trees. Noah had to gather wood by himself. That was a difficult task. It took longer than Noah had anticipated building an ark.

Lake Superior climate was too damp and too cold for Adam, Eva and Noah so they boarded Noah's ark to escape the damp and cold climate. Noah held a grudge. George wanted to leave the island. Noah would not let George board the ark because George had refused to chop down the red grape vines.

Too many animals snuck onto the ark so several species were thrown overboard to make room for Adam and Eva. Noah was afraid of snakes so he removed the plank from the ark. The snake could not slither up onto the ark. The snake did not have feet to jump or wings to fly so it could not get onto the ark. The Serpent snake and the species that were thrown overboard drowned and became extinct.

The ark floated eastward from Lake Superior through Lake Michigan, Lake Huron, Lake Erie, Lake Ontario and the St. Lawrence Seaway to the Atlantic Ocean. Noah knew to take that route because he discovered a Google map that belonged to *The King.* The map was buried in the ground next to the *Forbidden Tree.* Noah knew that he could follow the route that *The King* took. He could reverse the trip and end up on the west side of Emerald Island that was located in the English Channel.

Adam and Eva's youngest son Jonah fell over board when the St. Lawrence Seaway emptied in to the Atlantic Ocean He was lost at sea.

The ark reached the middle of the Atlantic Ocean. After three days they miraculously found Jonah.

Jonah was treading water trying to keep his head out of the water. Eva reached out to grab Jonah and pulled him onto the ark. They were all excited to be reunited. Noah asked Jonah how he survived in the Atlantic Ocean with no ark. Jonah told his story. "I was floating in the Atlantic Ocean treading water trying not to drown. I was exhausted and I began to sink. A huge wave caused me to float into a whale's open mouth. I was saved from drowning when I was swallowed by the large black and blue whale. I camped inside the whale's belly for three days and three nights. While inside the huge whale I found a pack of matches that was imprinted *Inferno* and a ream of paper with the letterhead *Zitsontush.* The matches and paper were dry. I was able to start a fire. Smoke built up inside the belly of the whale. Fortunately for me most of the smoke rose up into the whales spout. That caused the whale to choke and spew me out."

Timing was perfect. Jonah did not have to tread water for too long a time. Noah's ark passed by Jonah within two minutes after Jonah was spewed out of the whale's mouth. Adam looked out of the starboard side of the ark. He exclaimed "the whale is circling our ark." Cousin Ahab killed the whale for food and oil. No one starved on the ark and there was plenty of oil to burn to light the way at night.

Thanks to the light that shined bright at night, Noah was able to spot land. It was the continent of Europe. The ark passed by the Rock of Gibraltar as it entered the Mediterranean Sea. Adam and Eva disembarked the ark in Spain because the ark floated too far for Adam and Eva to disembark in Portugal. Adam and Eva were still only covered with a fig leaf.

People that lived on the continent laughed at Adam and Eva when they saw Eva's extremely huge round tush and the zits on Adam's tush.

A sensuous woman named *Bathsheba*, the *Adulteress* offered Eva clothing to cover her *tush*. She did not offer Adam clothing because she thought that the *zits* on Adam's *tush* were cute. .She wanted to stare at his *tush*. She offered to *shtoop* his brains out because her husband wasn't at home. Adam refused her offer because Eva was standing beside him. Eva stole some clothes from Bathsheba for Adam and herself. Fully clothed, they traveled east across Europe from Spain to France. They anticipated traveling to Italy and Russia.

Eva became pregnant in Spain. She gave birth to Kane and Abel in France.

Kane became a crop farmer and his younger brother Abel became a shepherd. Adam and Eva favored their younger son because he was very handsome and kind. Kane was ugly and nasty. Kane teased Abel. He called him a sissy because Abel had a soft job tending sheep and Kane had a hard job hoeing dirt to plant crops.

Kane was jealous of Abel so he threw a small pebble at Abel which knocked a tooth out of his mouth. Eva told Abel to put the tooth under the haystack pillow ton which he rested his head at night. Eva gave Abel one chocolate bar. She was the first tooth fairy of record.

That infuriated Kane even more. Kane attacked Abel and knocked out another tooth. Abel swallowed the tooth. It became lodged in his throat and he choked to death. That was the first killing of one man by another man.

Kane wandered throughout France and died when he fell on a stick that knocked out all of his teeth. He bled to death. That was the first killing of a man by accident.

Noah missed his parents Adam and Eva so he sailed away from Spain toward France. He moored his ark on the shore of Cannes, France and walked along the coast until he found his parents in Nice, a beautiful city in southern France on the Mediterranean Sea. Noah met and married Lorraine. Adam and Eva died. They were struck by lightning when they were skinny dipping in the Mediterranean Sea.

Noah and Lorraine continued traveling north to Versailles Gardens in France. They had a son Davy. He was a frail young boy with long curly sandy blonde hair.

CHAPTER IV

GRANDFATHER DAVY ZITSONTUSH MOYSHE'S 11TH GREAT GRANDFATHER

Davy had no friends so he made a toy to keep himself busy. Noah gave Davy three pieces of wood and Lorraine gave him a rubber band that she took out of the pony tail in her hair.

Grandfather Davy Zitsontush invented the sling shot. He placed acorns in to the rubber band and aimed them at a cherry tree in Versailles. He hit 50 out of 50 cherries. The cherries fell off the tree. Noah, Lorraine and Davy traveled east to Italy.

Approximately three hundred miles past Italy there was a beautiful town named Mountie Carlos in the country of Ocanom. It was located on the Mediterranean Sea.

The Phillysteins Army was at war with the Ocanom National Guard. The Phillysteins were attempting to annex Mountie Carlos. Twice a day for 40 days, Goliath, the champion of the Phillysteins Army, walked into the town and challenged the National Guard to send out a champion of their own to fight Goliath to decide the outcome in a single battle.

The entire National Guard was afraid of Goliath, a man the size of a Giant. Noah and Lorraine wanted to settle in the beautiful town but they were concerned about a Phillysteins victory.

Although Davy was frail they knew that he could be of help. The Prince of Ocanom promised to reward any man who could defeat Goliath

Little Davy Zitsontush and Giant Goliath confronted each other. Goliath wore armor covering his entire body. He wore a metal helmet on his head. He held a javelin in his right hand and a sword in his left hand.

Davy brought his sling shot, four acorns and a stone to the battle. He was dressed in a soft loin cloth covering his body. He did not wear a helmet on his head. Goliath laughed at the puny little boy and shouted that he would squash Davy with his feet and then cut off his *schmeckle* with the sword and throw the *schmeckle* into the Mediterranean Sea for the big fish to eat.

Davy said that he would run around Goliath three times, pace off 50 steps in front of him and then strike him dead. Goliath and the entire Phillysteins Army laughed. The Prince of Ocanom and all of the townspeople shuddered with fear. Noah and Lorraine were not concerned. If they were concerned no one would know it. No one saw them sweat. A man dressed in a black and white vertically striped jersey with a pink plastic whistle in his mouth stood between the two opponents. He blew the whistle, counted to three and shouted" let the battle begin". Goliath walked forward. Davy ran around Goliath three times then paced off 50 feet in front of the Giant. Goliath was too big of a Giant to move fast so Davy had plenty of time to circle him. Davy showed Goliath his pouch that held four acorns.

He hurled an acorn from his sling shot with all his might and hit Goliath on the right knee cap. Goliath writhed with pain. A second acorn hit Goliath's left knee cap. He began to cry louder. A third acorn knocked the javelin out of Goliath's right hand and a fourth acorn knocked the sword out of Goliath's left hand. Goliath had counted four acorns. Confident that Davy was out of acorns he picked up speed and he moved closer.

Davy had tricked Goliath. He did not show him the stone that he had hidden in his jock strap Davy reached into his shorts. Goliath and the Phillysteins laughed. They thought that Davy was playing with himself in the middle of the battle. Davy pulled out the stone and placed it into the sling shot. He flung the stone as hard as he could. The stone landed in the center of the Giant's forehead. Goliath fell on his face to the ground and he died instantly. Davy picked up Goliath's sword and cut off his tiny *schmeckle*, it was not proportional to the size of the Giant. He placed Goliath's *schmeckle* on the tip of the sword and showed it to the Phillysteins. They stopped laughing. One of the Phillysteins soldiers screamed "It's a *pitsel (tiny) schmeckle*". Then Davy flung Goliath's tiny *schmeckle* into the Mediterranean Sea. The minnows swam up to it and started to *kinibble.* The Phillysteins fled and were pursued by the Ocanom National Guard as far as Siberia in northeast Russia where the entire Phillysteins army froze to death. The Prince of Ocanom was true to his word. He built a house in Mountie Carlos for Noah and Lorraine.

Moyshe didn't believe that Adam and Eva or their children were his ancestors. *Bubby* insisted that they were his ancestors because they were the first people on earth to marry to have children. Therefore, everyone had to be their descendants.

Historians did find proof that Adam, Noah, Jonah and Davy shared the same last name Zitsontush but there were no records to prove their direct lineage.

Noah and Lorraine died after living happily ever after in Mountie Carlos.

Davy was introduced to Princess Bertha of Ocanom when he was gambling in the Mountie Carlos Casino. Davy and the Prince made a bet in a game of *Baccalaureate.* The wager was that the Prince would divorce the Princess of Ocanom if Davy won and Davy would join the Prince's National Guard if the Prince won. Davy won. Once again, The Prince was a man true to his word. The

Prince of Ocanom divorced Princess Bertha. She married her hero little Davy Zitsontush.

However, the Prince had a card up his sleeve. He banished Davy and Bertha from Ocanom. They traveled northwest to Suraleb, a small country ruled by King Aleb.

Suraleb was too small a country to have a strong army so many larger countries were always attacking. King Aleb kept getting migraine headaches from these attacks.

King Saul from the small country of Nilland told Aleb about Davy Zitsontush, the conqueror of Goliath.

He had heard that Davy and Bertha were banished from Ocanom. Davy had become a part time "hit man" to earn a living. He learned how to play the lyre so he took small gigs whenever possible. The sweet sounds from his lyre could cure headaches. Aleb summoned Davy and requested that Davy play some sweet soothing songs. He paid Davy to put a hit on the leaders of Aleb's enemies.

Davy was able to cure minor headaches, not migraines. Aleb's headaches became worse. Davy ran out of acorns and stones so he was useless with his slingshot.

Davy and Bertha were banished from East Suraleb because Aleb's headaches became worse. They decided to travel to West Suraleb. They had one son Avrohom.

CHAPTER V

AVROHOM ZITSONTUSH
MOYSHE'S 10ᵀᴴ GREAT GRANDFATHER

T he original Zitsontush family members were Nudniks. Everyone in Suraleb was a Nudnik. Avrohom Zitsontush was a Nudnik.

He was 6' 2" tall and proud of his well carved physique. As a farmer he toiled in the fields from 6:00 AM until 6:00 PM for 6 days a week. Sarah cooked chicken and served salad every evening for dinner. Because Avrohom ate chicken and salad for dinner and he toiled in the field every day, he was able to maintain his weight of 145 lbs. Long, curly brown hair kept getting in his eyes so he was constantly pushing it back over his head. He could see better when his hair didn't cover his eyes. Muscles developed on his arms because of the toiling in the field and pushing the long, curly hair over his head. Sarah was very beautiful with long blonde hair. She was very chubby, weighing in at 223 lbs.

According to Avrohom's Nudnik friends Shelly and Howie *The Little Bang Theory* explained the creation of the world. *The Little Bang Theory* stated that the universe was empty at the beginning of time. Everything began with a super massive very large tube of super glue. It bonded small rocks to form a huge rock. Then energy was created to break the huge rock. As time passed the rocks fell out of the sky due to gravitational forces. Depending on the size of the rocks many land formations landed in a great big body of water. The land formations were known as islands, countries and continents. The great big body of water became smaller bodies of water because the land formations dispersed sections of the large body of water. The combination of land and water became known as earth. We already know that Adam and Eva Zitsontush were the first people to live on earth. Nudniks believed in the *Little Bang Theory*.

Avrohom was a skeptical Nudnik. He was not convinced about The *Little Bang Theory*. He believed that The *Little Bang Theory* was hogwash because it couldn't be proven. He believed that earth had to be created by a *Supreme Being*. Avrohom was a proponent that a *Supreme Being* created the world in six days and rested on the seventh day. The seventh day of the week was to be known as the *Sabbath or Saturday, the day of rest.* The first day of the week was to be known as Sunday.

Avrohom was more satisfied with a religious, not a scientific theory for the creation of the earth. He was dissatisfied with the errant ways of his Nudnik neighbors. They worshipped wood idols, trees, birds and bees. The only faith they had was in the growth of their plants, trees and farmlands. Cows and chickens were more important than family. Nudniks did not accept any religion. Avrohom believed that his neighbors would flourish if they shared a common belief, a common religion.

Avrohom was a student of all religious beliefs. He agreed with other religious scholars that a *Supreme Being* had to have created the earth.

Avrohom founded the *Mensche* religion to preach this theory. He was to be known as the father of *Mensche* Religion. Avrohom was no longer a *Nudnik*.

Avrohom married Sara. They had a son Isaac. Sara was still alive when Avrohom married for the second time. He did not get a divorce so he would be known as a bigamist in modern day America.

Avrohom and his second wife Keturah had three sons. Their names were Curls, Lard and Schmoe. Avrohom was ridiculed by his business acquaintances because he was married to two wives at the same time and three of his sons had abnormal names. His first love Sara was his favorite wife. The embarrassment from his acquaintances led him to divorce Keturah. He decided to give a gift to his favorite wife and son. He gave everything that he owned to Sara and Isaac on the condition that Isaac continues to believe in the *Mensche* Religion. Eventually, the ridicule stopped.

Keturah and her three sons continued to be Nudniks just to spite Avrohom. He exiled them to Siberia because they adamantly refused to accept the *Mensche* Religion. They all froze to death in Siberia. Avrohom did not sit *Shiva* for Keturah and her three sons when they died. *Shiva* lasted seven days of which to mourn the death of a family member. A person did not work, play or ride cows during the *Shiva* period.

Just as Avrohom chose to worship *Supreme Being*, so did *Supreme Being* choose Avrohom to be his favorite Mensche. *Supreme Being* made an E*verlasting Covenant* with Avrohom and his descendants. "They would be the *chosen people.*"

Avrohom did not have a fountain pen. He could not write the covenant on paper. *Supreme Being* did not have a chisel. He could not engrave the covenant in stone. Avrohom could not remember the contents of the covenant. *Supreme Being* would not repeat the covenant to Avrohom. No one knew that there was a covenant.

When Avrohom died, Isaac buried him in the dark cave of Suraleb. Avrohom was buried with his wife Sara. In their wills they requested to be buried in the same plain wooden coffin that was to be held closed with wooden pegs. Sara had requested to be buried on top of Avrohom so that they would both be able to fit into one coffin.

Isaac inherited his father's farm lands and jewelry. He sold some of the jewelry. He became a wealthy jewelry merchant. He planted flowers on the farm lands. He sold the flowers. He became a wealthy florist. Isaac sat *Shiva* to mourn Avrohom and Sara.

Upon Avrohom's death, Isaac became the Chief Executive Officer and his wife Rebecca became the Chief Financial Officer of the *Mensche* Temple. Chief Financial Officer was a title only with no responsibilities because there were no funds in the "treasury".

Kings and Princes sought Isaac's friendship and advice when he was alive. The high regard in which he was held can be seen in the following Tovrah statement: "On the day that Isaac, CEO of *Mensche* Religion passes away, all the heads of the nations will stand in line and lament: "*Oy vey iz mir* (Woe be me) whose leader is dead. Woe to the caravan whose lead camel will be lost in the desert." The rest of the caravan followed the lead camel. Everyone became lost in the desert.

Isaac Zitsontush had continued in his father's footsteps when he was alive. He was a devout *Mensche*. Avrohom's son Isaac married Rebecca. Isaac was Moyshe's 9th Great Grandfather. Rebecca was barren and she was told by Dr. Max the Second that Isaac and she would never have children. There would be no one to continue the Zitsontush family name.

Isaac believed that if he prayed hard enough he and Rebecca would have a child. He prayed morning, noon and night. They shtooped every morning, noon and night. To reward Isaac and Rebecca for praying, *Supreme Being* blessed Isaac and Rebecca with three sons. Isaac and Sarah proved that Dr. Max the Second was wrong. The three sons were named Moses, Veissmuler and Bunyan. They were triplets. They were born six minutes apart. The boys did not look alike. Moses had blonde hair. Veissmuler had brown hair. Bunyan had red hair. The Zitsontush family name would survive because of the birth of the three sons.

The Zitsontush brothers Moses, Veissmuler and Bunyan were farmers in western Suraleb.

Isaac and Rebecca died on the same day. They died six minutes after the triplets were born. Isaac died first. Rebecca died six minutes later. The three brothers accepted *Mensche* Religion because it was the religion of their Grandfather Avrohom and their Father Isaac. The three boys sat *Shiva* for their parents. The three boys missed their parents. Six minutes after Isaac and Rebecca died the boys decided to move to a new community.

They had heard that there was a country of great opportunity. The country of Bupkis was west of Suraleb. Moses, Veissmuler and Bunyan packed their mules with food, clothing and SP50 sun tan lotion. They traveled west to Bupkis country, the land of opportunity. . It was not an easy trip to Bupkis.

CHAPTER VI

MOSES ZITSONTUSH
MOYSHE"S 8ᵀᴴ GREAT GRANDFATHER

Moses Zitsontush led his two brothers Veissmuler, Bunyan and their wives west across the Suraleb plateau. Although the plateau was a vast stretch of barren land, they never went hungry because they were smart farmers. They were able to devise methods to grow products in barren land. They planted fast growing carrots and lettuce for vegetables. They planted fast growing oranges. They drank freshly squeezed orange juice to stay hydrated. They had to squeeze the oranges by hand because they forgot to bring an extension cord for their food and fruit processor. They brought their cows so they would have beef to eat. They did not think ahead. They would not be able to ride the cows after the cows were eaten. Bunyan Zitsontush was a Boy Scout so he knew how to start a fire by holding a magnifying glass over a few pieces of grass. The hot sun piercing through the magnifying glass caused the grass to catch on fire. They needed fire to cook the beef.

When they tired from jogging across the plateau, they rode the cows that they had not eaten. Moses and his brothers reached the foot of *Sky High Mountain* and were stymied. There were no escalators to ascend the mountain. Escalators were not invented until 1859 in the State of Massachusetts in the United States of America. They ran to the top *of Sky High Mountain* and crossed over to Bupkis.

One of the mules was too stubborn to climb the mountain so Bunyan carried it.

CHAPTER VII

BUPKIS, EUROPE

B upkis, the land of opportunity is a small landlocked country in Eastern Europe contiguous to Suraleb on the east. It is bordered by Rustland to the north. Ukraine is to the south. Poland is to the west and Lithuania and Latvia is to the northwest.

Bupkis and Suraleb are separated by the *Sky High* Mountain Range.

Until the middle of the 20th century, the lands of modern-day Bupkis belonged to several countries. They were Klutzland, and Yutzland.

Bupkis War II (BWII or BW2) also known as the Second Bupkis War came shortly after the Great War known as Bupkis War I (BWI). The war lasted from 1612-1618. BWII lasted from 1639-1645. It was a global war that involved the vast majority of Europe's nations. Two opposing military alliances were formed. They were the Friendlies and the Unfriendlies. The war directly caused hundreds of deaths of civilians. Thirty- five soldiers died.

Klutzland and Yutzland were members of the Unfriendlies Alliance. These two countries dominated Bupkis from 1639-1645.

The Friendlies liberated Bupkis in 1646. Bupkis declared its independence in 1648.

The country of Bupkis has a current population of 150,000. Its capital is *Kishkapolis*. The capitol was formerly known as *Kish*. Bupkis is a Democratic country which allows male and female residents that are nine years or older to vote. The population is 55% *Mensche*, 30% Nudnik, 10% Klutz and 5% Yutz. The country has two official languages. They are Mensche and Kvetch. Mensche is the primary language. Previous to becoming a major city, *Kish* was a rural agricultural community. It was comprised of large forests and numerous small fertile farm lands.

The trees from the forests were grown for their lumber value. 30% of the lumber was exported to nearby towns and European countries. 20% were grown to be cut down and sold as Hanukah and Christmas trees. 40% were transported by carts to the *Swish River*. The trees floated down the *Swish River* to the lumber factory located in the small town of *Kish*. The lumber factory workers in *Kish* cut the trees into long slats of smooth lumber. 20% of the slats were used to build the 23 houses, one dry goods store, three saloons and one bank in the small town of *Kish*.

The balance of the lumber was used to produce various paper products. The process of producing paper consisted of five steps. First the lumber was cut into long slats. Second, the slats were soaked in long vats that were filled with water from the *Swish River*. Third, the dirt and other impurities from the *Swish River* were rinsed away before being turned into small chips of wood. Fourth, the chips were moved to the pulping factory. Fifth, the chips were turned into pulp for making various paper products.

Sometimes the paper was coated with fine clay to make it glossier and heavier. It was easier to print on glossy paper. That was how wrapping paper and wallpaper was made for ink patterns to be drawn on by hand. The inks were imported from India.

Farmers raised pigeons, chickens, pigs, horses and cows. The farmers grew grapes for producing *Kish* Merlot, the famous delicious *kosher* red wine. *Kish Mer*lot was the only libation sold in *Manny's Saloon* and *Mordecai's Tavern*. *Joe's Local Bar* featured Grape Sarsaparillas. Many farmers harvested corn and grain for animal feed and for making *Kishka* (pig's intestine filled with beef, corn and grain).

20% of *Kish Merlot* was distributed to the nearby towns. 20% was sold to *Manny's Saloon*. 10% was sold *to Mordecai's Tavern* and the balance was reserved for the local vintners' personal consumption.

30% of *kishka* was exported to neighboring countries. The balance was eaten by the local farmers and town folks. *Kishka* and corn were the most favorite side dishes to accompany the farmers' delicious breakfast, lunch and dinner entrées. Chickens were raised to provide breakfast scrambled eggs and kosher entrées for Friday night dinners. Pigs were raised to provide bacon as a side dish for the kosher meals. Bacon was served for every breakfast, lunch and dinner. The pigs' intestines were used to make *kishka*. Cows were raised to provide skim milk. Horses were raised to provide beef for stuffing the *kishka*.

Cows pulled carts to carry products to local market. Whenever the cows were being milked, which was quite often, the female children of the farmers had to pull the carts. The farmers' wives couldn't pull the carts. They were too busy milking the cows. The farmers couldn't pull the carts. They were too busy sitting on their ass in the morning while overseeing the laborers do their chores. The farmers were too busy in the afternoon sitting on their *ass* while drinking and gambling at *Manny's Saloon.*

The pigeons carried advertising pamphlets to promote *Kish's* products. Many times the pigeons couldn't fly because there were too many heavy pamphlets attached to their scrawny legs. When they could fly there were times that they started flight toward their destinations and they could only go short distances because they tired from flapping their wings. There was too much weight on their scrawny legs so they fell down. The pigeons crashed into the *Swish River* and they drowned. The pamphlets got all wet. The ink came off the flyers and the *Swish River* became contaminated.

It took several months to decontaminate the river. That happened more often than not.

Despite the problem, the rural community grew and became a major city. That was due to the growth of the manufacturing and export business. The Zitsontush family and their neighbors contributed to the growth. The city *Kish* changed its name to *Kishkapolis*. It was named for the famous Bupkis *Kish Merlot* wine and *Kishka* food.

The *Swish River* is the longest waterway in Bupkis. It originates at the top of *Sky High Mountain* and flows down the mountain toward the farm lands. The small streams of the *Swish River* enrich the fertile soil. The river continues to flow toward the center of the city of Kishkapolis providing power for many factories.

Kurtsville is the second largest city in the country of Bupkis. It is located two miles down the river from *Kishkapolis*. The shorter trees that were not taken for the factories in *Kish*kapolis were taken for use in the factories in Kurtsville. The shorter trees were cut into narrow slats to manufacture small carts. The balance of the trees continued down the river to the waste factory in the town of *Gornisht,* the third largest town in the country of Bupkis. The workers in the waste factory cut the trees into small pieces and put them into baskets that were placed into the *Swish River* to float further down the river to the town of *Brennholz.* Storekeepers in the town of *Brennholz* took the baskets out of the *Swish River* and they sold the small pieces of wood to customers to burn the wood in their cast iron stoves. *K*ishka was made in the cast iron stoves. The baskets of wood sold for twenty-five cents. That included a deposit of two cents for the basket. The basket was returned to the storekeeper. The deposit was returned to the customer. The empty basket was returned to the waste factory to be reused.

That process was the forerunner of the modern day concept of *recycling.*

Freizeitpark Village, the smallest town in the country of Bupkis is in the resort area of *Aquah* located one quarter mile east of Lake *Aquah,* a light aqua color body of water, famous for carp and pike fishing. During the summer swimming and large white sandy beaches attracted many people. The mayor of the Village boasted of Bupkis's largest amusement park. It was located in the center of the Village. There was a large merry-go- round and roller coaster. There were no other rides. The only ice cream stand in the town of Freizeitpark *Village* was located in the amusement park so admission to the park was free. Ice cream cost 20 cents per scoop. The park was open only during the summer months. Freizeitpark Village had a population of 1,545. The population increased to 17,500 during the summer months because many of the wealthy Bupkis residents from the nearby towns vacationed in Freizeitpark Village for recreation and relaxation.

Moses, Veissmuler and Bunyan could see the entire country of Bupkis from the top of *Sky High* Mountain. They saw the small town of Kish and decided to meet there when they reached the bottom of the mountain.

There are several streams at the top of *Sky High* Mountain. The streams flow down the west side of the mountain. Veissmuler with his wife Jane, their son Junior and pet Koala Bear swam down the largest stream. The stream flowed into the *Swish River.* Bunyan and his wife Lucette rented a canoe at the top of the mountain. Moses and his wife Zippora walked down the mountain. The families joined each other in the small town of *Kish. T*he town is located along side of the *Swish River* in the country of Bupkis.

Moses and Bunyan bought an acre of farmland and an acre of forest on the outskirts of *Kish.*

They decided that Moses would work the good earth and Bunyan would be a lumberjack and cut down and grow trees. Veissmuler decided to teach swimming in the *Swish River.* The Zitsontush brothers brought "birds and bees" from Suraleb. Their wives insisted that they keep the "birds and bees" in their cages and "sex" in their jeans. The husbands agreed! However, Junior did not agree. Veissmuler and his family bought a cabin on *Growth Street* in the town of *Kish.* There was a small epidemic that began when Junior lived on Growth Street. He began to *shtoop* several maidens that lived on Growth Street. Many grown men became jealous of Junior so they began to have sex with their unmarried female cousins. Several of the young girls became pregnant. The population on Growth Street grew from 8 to 14 people within one year. The population grew geometrically. Within 3 years 73 people lived on *Growth Street*. The "birds and the bees" epidemic continued for many years. The population grew to 3,675 people. Many *Kish* residents blamed the entire Zitsontush family for the "birds and bees" epidemic.

Veissmuler charged 35 cents per swim lesson. He was not able to earn enough money to support his family so he worked part time with Moses during the spring season on the farm land. He worked full time with Bunyan during the fall season cutting trees. During the winter season he sold Hanukah and Christmas trees. It was too cold to swim in the *Swish River* during the fall, winter and spring seasons. Veissmuler continued to give swimming lessons during the summer season.

Moses and Zippora gave birth to one son Ashe.

CHAPTER VIII

ASHE ZITSONTUSH
MOYSHE'S 7TH GREAT GRANDFATHER

Ashe Zitsontush inherited a substantial amount of money from the Zitsontush Family fortunes. He had the opportunity to pursue his life- long ambition. He studied diligently at Bupkis University to become a nurse. There were no male nurses in Bupkis. He knew that there would be a great opportunity for him to be of value to his new home country. He could have retired on the amount of money that he inherited but it was more important for him to stay active and help his Bupkis neighbors.

Bupkis was involved in the 3 Years War in Europe.

Ashe enlisted in the Bupkis Army. The war was fought between a Five Country Alliance of Francland, Rustland Swedtland, Austland and Swisland. The Five countries fought against the Alliance of Yutzland and Klutzland. In Germland the Seven Years War was known as the 'First Viral War'. Germland was an independent country. It was not a member of any Alliance.

Yutzland and Klutzland had previously invaded and occupied Bupkis. The Yutz and Klutz feared invasion from Germland so they formed an alliance to invade and wipe out the Germs.

The Yutz-Klutz Alliance officially went to war against the Five Country Alliance and Germland.

A Euro Treaty was signed by neutral countries. The Treaty prevented them from being sucked in to helping either Alliance. Francland was the largest and wealthiest nation in Europe. With The two Alliances at war, the Francs financed the Five Country Alliance to protect their own interests. They were financed enough to strike and defeat the Yutz-Klutz Alliance and Germland.

Rustland, an independent country was planning a similar initiative against the Yutz-Klutz Alliance. General Ruffenready of the Yutz-Klutz Alliance was aware of the plotting. He initiated war against Rustland and Germland in an attempt to gain an advantage over his enemies. He wanted to defeat Germland and Rustland before the Five Country Alliance could mobilize. General Ruffenready also wanted to seize more land for the Yutz-Klutz Alliance.

General Ruffenready attacked Rustland to procure more land. He attacked Francland to take over the Franc banks. With the victory over Francland he seized the financial resources to set up his planned campaign. He occupied the capitol of Francland, He accepted the surrender, incorporating their troops and sucking huge funds out of the country. The bankers controlled the capitol. They were willing to surrender because General Ruffenready promised them that he would not cut off their *schmeckles.*

The Five Country Alliance attacked the Yutz-Klutz Alliance with the hope of controlling Bupkis. General Ruffenready and his army were able to stop the Alliance at the border. The Five Country Alliance lost the Battle of Bupkis.

There were several battles in Bupkis. In the Battle of Rolling General Ruffenready was wounded by an errant stone causing severe injury to his kneecap. He limped off the battlefield. Without the leadership of General Ruffenready, the Yutz-Klutz Alliance was defeated by the Five Country Alliance's relief forces at the Battle of Rolling. General Ruffenready and his army were forced to retreat out of Bupkis.

General Ruffenready was in the care of Nurse Ashe Zitsontush. Ashe was a good nurse. He assisted several Paramedics to save General Ruffenready's knee from bleeding profusely. It took months to heal so General Ruffenready sank into self pity. Ashe continued to put iodine and band aids on General Ruffenready's knee. He nursed the General to good health. General Ruffenready recuperated and returned to Bupkis to defeat the Five Country Alliance at the Battle of Stronghold. The Yutz-Klutz Alliance gained complete control of Bupkis. To celebrate his victory, General Ruffenready sent two of his guardsmen to purchase a new food that was baked in Italiland restaurants. They brought back hundreds of dozens of huge family size pizzas. General Ruffenready was the first person of record to host *a Pizza Party. Kish Merlot* wine and water from the contaminated *Swish River* quenched the soldiers' thirst. The water was boiled to remove the impurities.

General Ruffenready was very thankful to Nurse Ashe. He had the authority to reward Ashe with a Doctorate in Medicine and He did. Nurse Ashe Zitsontush became Dr. Ashe Zitsontush when the war ended. Dr. Ashe Zitsontush was honorably discharged from the army. He became a full time doctor in *Kish,* Bupkis.

Ashe was a compassionate man. He was not a *khazer (greedy person).* Dr. Ashe Zitsontush did not charge for office visits. He only charged for house calls. Ashe specialized in treating rare diseases. He treated people that had *Zits disease.* His patients complained of Zits on their *punim* (face) and *tush.* He travelled all over Bupkis to make house calls for his patients. He did not ask for money as payment because his patients were poor. He accepted vegetables for payment only if his patients offered them.

An annual doctor's convention was held in *Kish.* Dr. Ashe Zitsontush was introduced to Dr. Trey Goodman, a Family specialist. He told Ashe about the charity work that he did in the *Sky High* Mountain Range. The *Sky High* people had a *Zits* problem on their tush. The disease spread rampantly throughout the Mountains. Dr. Trey Goodman didn't know how to contain the disease. Ashe agreed to help him. The two doctors traveled together to the Sky High Mountains to cure the people that were contaminated with *Zits*. Ashe taught Trey how to cure the disease.

Ashe had to return to *Kish* to help his friend Farmer Brown. Farmer Brown owned a *wholly cow* that had a Zits problem on its *tush.* The cow was having a difficult time. Its tail could not scratch the itch on its *tush.* The cow had another problem. It was pregnant. The cow was having a difficult time giving birth to its calf. Besides being *a Zits specialist,* Ashe was a *veterinarian.*

Trey came with Ashe to help. He held half of the *Wholly Cow* to steady its head. Ashe held the other half. The calf was born. It came out of the cow's *tush.* The cow's owner Farmer Brown saw the calf emerge from the *tush.* He screamed "Holy Cow". That is how the saying became popular. Dr. Trey Goodman was very impressed with Dr. Ashe Zitsontush so he remained in *Kish.* The two doctors set up a partnership. They named it *Ashe-Trey Veterinarian & Family Practice.* The partnership flourished. *Ashe-Trey* owned a lot of vegetables that their poor farmer patients gave them as payment for their services. Trey was married to Louise. They had a son Oliver and a daughter Janet. The children carried the vegetables to market to sell them to the people in *Kish.* Oliver sold the vegetables and Janet collected the money. They put the proceeds in the Ashe-Trey Partnership.

Oliver and Janet learned how to swim. They took lessons from Veissmuler. He trained them to swim good enough to earn a spot on the Bupkis Swim Team. They competed in the European Olympics. There were twenty contestants. Janet and Oliver finished in eighteenth and nineteenth place, respectively.

They competed the following year. Janet finished in 14th place, Oliver finished in fifteenth place. Although they improved, the siblings went back to selling vegetables for *Ashe-Trey.*

Janet and Oliver needed money so Ashe convinced Trey to let Janet and Oliver retain the proceeds. They were smart children. Janet and Oliver bought baskets with the proceeds and they sold the baskets to the storekeepers in the town of *Brennholz*. The business flourished. They saved enough money to live happily ever after even though neither one found anyone to marry. The town's people gossiped about Oliver and Janet. They thought it was weird that a brother and sister lived together. They never found a companion to marry. Fortunately, she never got pregnant.

Ashe married Aliza. They gave birth to triplets. One daughter was named Adriana and two sons were named Schlemiel and Mazel. They were good children because they helped their mother Aliza with the household chores. Schlemiel washed the laundry. Mazel ironed the laundry and Adriana folded the laundry.

Adriana was more beautiful than a mythical Greek Goddess. At the age of 14 years old she married Goldan Mann, a 70 years old wealthy land and mine owner. He was a Nudnik. Adriana was a *Mensche*. They respected each other religion. They never had children. She was too young and he was too old to have children.

The *Sky High* Mountain Range was on the eastern end of Goldan's land. He owned coal mines in the *Sky High* Mountains. Goldan was already a wealthy man before gold and silver were discovered in his coal mines. He employed three men to extract silver from the mountains and pan for gold in the streams that flowed from the mountains into the *Swish River*

CHAPTER IX

SCHLEMIEL ZITSONTUSH MOYSHE'S 6TH GREAT UNCLE

S chlemiel was not very lucky and he was not very smart. He constantly bragged to many men that Adriana married a "gold mine". The men were annoyed by Schlemiel's bragging. They knew that Schlemiel was not very smart so they told him a story about *Rumpelspinster,* a woman that spun straw into gold. Schlemiel borrowed money from his wealthy brother-in-law to buy a farm. He grew vines for grapes and he seeded his land to grow grass, nothing else. Schlemiel harvested the grass and let it dry in the extremely hot sun for three years. He bought an expensive spinning wheel from *Rumpelspinster* to spin the straw into gold. Schlemiel was too busy spinning straw so he never had time to date any women. He never married. Schlemiel *was* a real *schlemiel* (unlucky jerk). He kept spinning the straw. It didn't turn into gold. He ran out of straw after three years. Schlemiel was determined to make gold. He grew more grass. He harvested it and let it dry in the hot sun for three years. He spun straw and produced straw. He tried again to spin the straw into gold. Six years later there was still no gold so he burned all of the straw. Schlemiel was too busy spinning straw so he ignored planting the grape vines. His water hose was too short to reach the vines He tried to extract water from the *Swish River.* Eventually the vines stopped growing. Schlemiel still wanted gold so he began panning for it in the *Swish River.*

He was not smart enough to know that the *Swish River* was too deep to pan for gold. His friend Cole Miner had a golden idea. He found a stream that was five hundred feet upstream from the *Swish River.* Gold landed in his pans before it reached Schlemiel's spot.

Schlemiel was certainly a *schlemiel.* He had an abundance of bad luck. His left thumb was severed from his hand when it got stuck in the spinning wheel. He developed hemorrhoids from sitting on his tush too long when he spun the straw. No matter how hard he tried, the straw never turned to gold. It only turned to *drek* (crap).

His twenty cows dried up and couldn't produce milk. They died from being dehydrated. He was so upset that he kicked the empty metal milk bucket and he stubbed his left big toe. The toe became black and blue. It swelled to the size of a golf ball. Assuming that the swelling would go down, he did not seek medical advice. Gangrene set in and his left foot was amputated.

He developed *hoof and mouth disease.* He attracted the disease from his dead cows. Huge terrible sores festered on his *tush.* The *hoof and mouth disease* spread to cows that were owned by other farmers. The cows died of the disease. Schlemiel was responsible for causing the *first hoof and mouth disease* epidemic of record. He wasn't smart enough to take the dead cows out of the hot sun. They rotted in the heat. Their bodies could not be used for meat to stuff into pig's intestines to make *kishka.* He certainly had no luck!

Goldan and Adrianna loved each other very much. Sadly, she became ill. No doctor in Bupkis could cure her rare disease.

She traveled to Tibet to seek a "cure". She died in Tibet; the "cure" killed her. Goldan became depressed when Adriana died. He was 98 years old and no longer capable of overseeing his fortunes.

He did not have any heirs. His only relatives were Schlemiel and Mazel. Goldan did not have faith in Schlemiel to protect his fortunes. He trusted Mazel.

Goldan knew that Schlemiel was unlucky and that he was a fool who didn't know *his tush* from a hole in the ground. He would probably pan for gold in the streams, find gold in his pan, not watch where he was walking and he would probably trip over his own feet. The gold would probably fall out of the pans and land in the deep *Swish River*.

Schlemiel was panning for gold one day when he "got lucky". He found gold in his pan. Then his "luck" ran out.

He did not watch where he was walking. He tripped over his own feet and the gold fell out of the pan and landed in the deep *Swish River*. Goldan had predicted it. He gave all of his fortunes to Mazel.

CHAPTER X

MAZEL ZITSONTUSH
MOYSHE'S 6TH GREAT GRANDFATHER

Mazel, unlike his brother Schlemiel, was very intelligent and very lucky. He protected Goldan from losing his fortunes. Schlemiel begged Mazel for help. Mazel told Schlemiel that he did not have to repay the loan that Goldan gave him. He knew that Schlemiel was unlucky enough to lose any money that Mazel might give him. Mazel did feel sorry for Schlemiel so he bought the spinning wheel and the grape vineyard from him. Schlemiel laughed at Mazel for buying the "worthless" spinning wheel and barren vineyard. Although Mazel was upset with Schlemiel for his remarks, he could not let his brother starve.

Mazel replanted the grape vines and they flourished. He discovered how to spin the charred straw back into hay. He sold the hay to other farmers. They fed their horses and cows with the hay. Mazel made a lot of money from the spinning wheel that produced hay. Schlemiel became despondent because of Mazel's good fortune. He frequented Manny's Tavern and drank gallons of *Kish* Merlot every week. It was the *Kish* Merlot that Mazel produced.

Ironically, the grapes for the *Kish* Merlot that Schlemiel drank were grown on the farm that he sold to Mazel. Eventually, Schlemiel drank himself to death.

Mazel was thankful to *Supreme Being* for his good luck. He promised to attend *Mensche* Temple every Sabbath and celebrate every *Mensche* Holy Day.

Mensche life is marked by numerous Holy Days in which adherents take time out of their everyday lives to stop work and focus on *Supreme Being* and his commandments.

The history of *Mensche* Religion is full of incredible stories. According to the Tovrah (History Book), the Holy Days are important for *Mensche* of all generations. The purpose of most of the Holy Days and festivals in *Mensche* Religion is to recall *Supreme Being's* teachings. Observance of the Holy Days is the most important aspects of the *Mensche* faith.

Observing Holy Days and festivals help to keep tradition alive and contribute to a sense of belonging. The most important *Mensche* Holy Days are the Sabbath, Rushinannualy and Yom Ruppik. It is forbidden to work on any of these days. *Mensche* observe the Holy Day that celebrates "New Planting of the Trees". It is the only Mensche Holy Day that it is mandatory to work because every *Mensche* that owns a forest must begin to plant trees on this day to replace the trees that were cut down the previous year. The trees that were used for Hanukah trees and Christmas trees and lumber had to be replaced.

Hanukah is the miracle of success over the more powerful enemies of the *Mensche*.

Rush Inannually is the *Mensche* New Year.

Yom Ruppik is the most solemn *Mensche* Holy Day. *Mensche* pray to *Supreme Being* for forgiveness of their sins of the previous year.

Mazel married Adela, a loving woman. They moved to Misktown, the capital of Suraleb. They had a son Meshulam.

CHAPTER XI

MESHULAM ZITSONTUSH
MOYSHE'S 5ᵀᴴ GREAT GRANDFATHER

Meshulam Zitsontush was born in Misktown. He attended Misktown Free Trade School where he learned how to operate a printing press. He graduated in two years and he became an apprentice to Johannes Gluten, a wealthy owner of the Gluten Printing Press Company in Misktown, Suraleb. Meshulam was a hard worker. Gluten had two presses. He only needed one press to accommodate the printing orders that he received from the Misktown Daily News. John Newsman, the owner of Newsworthy Printing Company moved his business from Lotis, Suraleb to Misktown. John was very competitive. Gluten's business decreased. He had to find a way to increase his income.

Gluten trusted Meshulam so he offered him an opportunity to lease the second press. Meshulam had to promise that he would not open a Printing Press business in Misktown. Gluten helped Meshulam dismantle the second press for ease of shipment.

Meshulam took the parts to *Kish*. He had a major problem. He could not afford to buy or rent a building to start his business.

Meshulam was an intelligent man. He learned many things about business and financing when he attended Misktown Free Trade School.

He remembered reading in the Newsworthy newspaper that Norman Rosinsky was a wealthy lumber factory owner in *Kish*, Bupkis. Norman was not a smart man. He was a lucky man. His Uncle Louis died and he bequeathed the lumber factory to Norman. Meshulam sent Norman a letter via carrier pigeon requesting a meeting. They had the meeting. Meshulam determined that Norman was a lazy and greedy man so he convinced Norman to invest in a new Printing business to be located in *Kish*. The clincher of the deal was that Meshulam would run the printing business and provide the printing press. Norman knew that Meshulam was leasing the press. That didn't matter to him. Norman was satisfied that he would not have to lift a finger to work. His only responsibility was to finance the startup and future growth of the business. Norman saw an opportunity to become wealthier without having to work. They became partners and formed A&N Printing Company. They bought an empty stretch of land alongside the *Swish River* that was adjacent to Norman's lumber business. They built a factory building on the land for the printing business. Misktown Free Trade School was worth every penny that Meshulam didn't have to pay for his free education.

Paper is made from pulp that comes from lumber. Norman's lumber business manufactured the paper that was sold to A&N Printing Company. Norman made more money because A&N Printing Company became the lumber business's largest customer. Meshulam married Leticia. They had twin boys, Solomon and Samson.

Solomon was a wise man and Samson was a strong man

Norman did not have any children. He was never married. When he died he bequeathed the lumber business and his ownership of the printing business to his partner Meshulam. The lumber business and the printing business were very successful. Meshulam was not a greedy man. He was a very good business man. His printing business produced advertising pamphlets that he and other business men in the community used very often.

Meshulam determined that Hanukah wrapping paper, Christmas wrapping paper and wallpaper manufacturing were very lucrative businesses. The lumber business produced the papers and the printing business was able to imprint the designs on the papers. Meshulam was the most successful business man in *Kish*. At the age of 20 years old Solomon and Samson joined their father in business. The three Zitsontush men were able to make the businesses more profitable. They consolidated the three businesses and formed Zitsontush Family Company. They owned the lumber business and the printing business. They bought a tree farm that was located in rural *Kish*.

CHAPTER XII

SAMSON ZITSONTUSH
MOYSHE'S 4TH GREAT UNCLE

S amson, the strong son operated the lumber business. He was able to carry and move more lumber than any of his factory workers. The employees respected Samson because he set a good example for them. Samson was not a lazy man. He worked the same long hours that his employees worked. He knew that hard work would pay off. Samson realized that the lumber company was not operating at full capacity even though everyone was working diligently.

Samson and his competitors transported lumber by ponies. The ponies were not very strong so they could only pull a limited amount of lumber. There were no grown horses available throughout Bupkis. The grown horses would have been able to pull more lumber.

Samson rented the fastest carrier pigeon in *Kish* to send a message to Solomon. message. He wrote: "The largest tree farmer in rural *Kish* had just died. His widow was going to sell the tree farm. Samson wanted to offer her a fair price so that they would own more lumber that could be converted into paper.

The horses would not be strong enough to pull the lumber so he wanted to buy *blue oxen.* They were the strongest animals that could pull the carts fully loaded with lumber and Bunyan would be able to use the *blue oxen* on his tree farm".

Solomon was a wise man so sent the following message to Samson "I AGREE!"

Samson bought the tree farm and the *blue oxen.* He and his employees worked harder. The factory was operating at full capacity. Samson sent the good news via carrier pigeon to Solomon. Solomon sent another message to Samson: "Give the employees a raise. Pay them 3 cents an hour more and buy the empty building and equipment that is next door." Samson gave the employees 3 cents an hour more. Samson bought the additional property and equipment. He hired more employees. The business increased and the community prospered because unemployment decreased. Solomon returned to *Kish* to help his brother.

Bunyan thanked his brothers for buying the *blue oxen.* He was able to send his brothers more lumber faster. Everyone prospered. The three Zitsontush brothers paid their employees higher wages. They employed additional workers to cut down trees and work in the lumber factory, wallpaper factory and printing businesses. More printing presses, lumberjack tools and inks were needed. The Zitsontush brothers bought as many local products as possible to operate their businesses. Their friend Byron Slomisky bought raw material to produce ink. The Zitsontush Brothers financed Slomisky to buy a factory to produce more inks. That created more jobs in *Kish.*

CHAPTER XIII

SOLOMON ZITSONTUSH
MOYSHE'S 4ᵀᴴ GREAT GRANDFATHER

Meshulam was still alive. He was proud of his three sons Solomon, Samson and Bunyan.

Bunyan operated the tree farm, Samson operated the lumber company and Solomon operated the printing and wallpaper businesses. Meshulam was retired and bored staying home and reading the newspaper that his company printed so he helped Bunyan. Meshulam worked three days a week. His only responsibility was to count the trees that were loaded onto the carts. The trees were placed in the *Swish River* for transportation to the lumber factory.

Meshulam and Leticia died a natural death caused by old age. Moyshe's 4ᵗʰ Great Uncles Samson and Bunyan and 4ᵗʰ Great Grandfather Solomon continued to operate the Zitsontush Family Company. The town of *Kish* grew rapidly. It became the largest town in Bupkis. The name of the town changed to *Kishkapolis* and it became the capital of the country.

Solomon, the wise man knew that he could buy products for the Zitsontush businesses cheaper if he went direct to the sources. He traveled throughout Asia, India and Europe to buy raw materials that he could import for use in manufacturing wallpaper. He imported grass cloths and silks from China. He imported tapestries from France. He imported various textiles from Spain and inks from India.

Solomon needed employees to help him. He offered his employees and other workers time and a half pay to travel with him. The people that were not working in the lumber factory jumped at the opportunity to earn forty cents an hour. They only earned minimum wages at their current jobs.

Solomon asked a few of his younger cousins to travel with him. They were young so he could pay them under the table or he would not have to pay them. He only had to give them shelter and feed them. Cousin Etude was a language interpreter. Solomon visited many famous landmarks during his travels as a fabric merchant. He marveled at the beauty of the *Taj Mahal* a white marble mausoleum that was built in1632-1643 to house the tomb of Mumtaz Mahal, wife of Shah Jahan. It is located on the southern bank of Yamuna River in the city of Agra in India. He walked through the domed marble tomb and the beautiful Gardens leading to two red-stone buildings surrounded by a crenellated wall (wall with holes along the top through which to shoot guns) on three sides. He contacted ink manufacturers in India. They developed multitudes of color inks and different hues of black inks.

Solomon rode mules along the 5,000 miles *Great Wall of China*. He had packed mules with water filtered from Lake *Aquah, Kish Merlot* wine, bacon from *Kish* pigs, chickens, oranges and corn from *Kish* farms and uncooked kishka. Cousin Schlomo was the cook. He fried the bacon and boiled the water on the surface of the Great Wall that would be scorching hot from the torrid sun. He made chicken soup and kishka with the boiled water. Cousin Attila arm wrestled the chief warlord and won. His victory saved everyone from being slaughtered by the warlords.

Solomon met many local people working in the rice paddies of *China*. He explained to them the process for manufacturing Hanukah and Christmas wrapping paper and wallpaper. They taught him a new way to process the rice, silk and grass to be applied to wallpaper.

Solomon experienced the fine music, food and nightlife of *Palermo, Italy*. Cousin Daniel taught him to dance so that he could smooch with many Signora, the attractive young women. He was far away from home so he did not fear that anyone would discover his indiscretions He swam in the *Mediterranean Sea* butt naked with many of the Signora*s*. Solomon ran in front of the bulls during the *Running of the Bulls in Pamplona, Spain.* It was an Event that originated in the 14th century. Cousin Lummox waived a red flag in front of the lead bull's face to divert him from getting too close to Solomon.

Solomon viewed the *Bastille in Paris, France.* He envisioned the imprisonment of the Yutz-Klutz revolutionaries. When he reached the *Red Sea* there were no boats to rent so he waited for a strong storm to part the sea so that he could walk *to Egypt.* He was able to rent a boat in *Egypt* so he traveled along the *Nile River* looking for baskets to hold the inks from *India.* He found one basket stuck along the river bank but they could not use it to carry the inks. The basket had a baby inside. Attila wanted to throw the basket back into the river to see how fast it would float down stream. Solomon was more compassionate. He put the basket in the boat. He decided to take the baby with him to *Kishkapolis.* Cousin Schlomo, the cook prepared milk from the cows to feed the baby. The insides of the *kishka were mashed for baby food* and broth was made from the chicken soup to feed the baby. Solomon brought the baby to Little *Annie's Orphanage for Unwanted Babies.* The baby grew up to be a *Kishkapolis* politician and he led the Reform *Mensche* in their pursuit to gain representation in the Nudnik Congress.

Solomon was the most knowledgeable of the Zitsontush family because of his travels.

He returned to *Kishkapolis* and the Zitsontush Family Companies. Bunyan only wanted to manage and own the tree farm. The three brothers agreed that Bunyan would own the tree farm and Solomon and Samson would own the lumber, wallpaper and printing businesses. Bunyan's Business was separated from the Zitsontush Family Company. It was a fair deal for everyone. Bunyan was successful because his brothers bought more trees from Bunyan for the Zitsontush Family Company.

Solomon shared his travel experiences with Samson. They combined Solomon's new knowledge and Samson's continued hard work to make the businesses even more successful.

Bunyan, Solomon and Samson earned a great amount of money. They were satisfied with their wealth. They were not *khazers*. The three brothers donated to many charities and needy businesses and individuals. Unlike their ancestors, the Zitsontush brothers chose to share their wealth. The Zitsontush Brothers were well respected in Kishkapolis.

Samson was touring the lumber factory on a Sabbath, day. He was not supposed to work on the Sabbath. He was *kibitzing* (chatting) with the factory manager. The manager told him that the factory floor was slippery because water from the *Swish River* splashed onto the floor. Samson did not watch where he was walking. The manager shouted "watch out, be careful." Samson was not careful. He slipped on some wet saw dust and he fell into the *Swish River*. One of the logs floating in the river hit him on the head and he drowned.

Solomon was sad, but not too sad; he inherited the entire Zitsontush Family Company.

Solomon married Vera and they had a son Mendel. Solomon died of a broken heart three months after Vera died. She was ill for one year with a rare disease. Pimples that formed on her ass broke and caused a terrible rash that became infected. There was no cure for the rash that was caused by the broken pimples.

CHAPTER XIV

MENDEL ZITSONTUSH
MOYSHE'S 3ᴿᴰ GREAT GRANDFATHER

Mendel retired before he inherited the Zitsontush Family Company from his father Solomon. He was *a khazer*. Mendel came out of retirement. He accumulated more *gelt* (money) than he could ever spend .He traveled further east in China than Solomon had traveled. Mendel learned more about the Chinese Wallpaper. The Chinese had discovered a newer use of silk to be converted into softer fine "string" wallpaper.

Mendel pondered. "How could he exploit these new discoveries?" He got more involved with operating the wallpaper manufacturing business. He envisioned another opportunity to satisfy his greed. He imported the "new" Chinese wallpaper and he learned how to manufacture it faster and cheaper so he began manufacturing Chinese "string" wallpaper. He had a large ego so he named this division of the Zitsontush Family Company, *Mendel's Wallpaper Manufacturers*. Mendel was the largest employer in *Kishkapolis*. He became Mayor of the city and he controlled all policies that governed businesses. A Business Tax was established. Many merchants could not afford the taxes so they closed their businesses and they moved to other cities. Mendel took advantage of the situation. He bought many vacant properties that were abandoned by the merchants. They found it necessary to leave *Kishkapolis*. Mendel was able to get the Business taxes lowered so he rented the properties to new tenants that could afford the lower taxes.

Mendel became the largest property owner in *Kishkapolis*. He resigned his position as Mayor because he knew that he would not win a second term. It did not matter to him. He had already accomplished what he intended to accomplish. He became even more successful than his ancestors. He was more disliked than anyone else in the community. But he didn't care!

Mendel discovered that he could distribute his wallpaper product to retail stores all over Bupkis. By cutting out the "middle man" (the distributor) Mendel could make a larger profit. He was very successful as a manufacturer and a retailer.

Mendel married Fiona. They had twin sons. Melek was born three minutes later than Midas. Upon Mendel's death, Melek and Midas inherited the Zitsontush Family Company.

Midas chose to lead an easy life. He collected rent money from the larger properties and lived off his portion of the rents collected. The manufacturing business was of no interest to him. He was too lazy to work.

Midas was Moyshe's 2nd Great Uncle. He never married because he preferred dating and *shtooping* different women, more than three per week. He stayed home and counted his money when he wasn't drinking in the local bars or *shtooping* women. Midas was a very greedy man. Melek was not a greedy man. Midas hoarded his wealth. He did not put any improvements into his properties. He was a slum landlord. Melek decided to operate the wallpaper business and manage the smaller properties. The income from the smaller properties and the income from the business was more than Melek needed. Melek agreed that his brother Midas could own and operate the larger properties. Eventually Melek bought his brother's portion of ownership in the Zitsontush Family Company because Midas only wanted money. Melek overpaid but it didn't matter to him. He was not greedy.

Midas tried to *shtoop* his brother Melek's wife Marianna. She was too embarrassed to tell Melek or the authorities. Midas drank a glass of *Kish Merlot* wine every evening at dinner time. One evening Marianna put some sleeping pills in his wine. That night she sneaked into his bedroom. He was sound asleep so she cut off his *schmeckle* and threw it into the Swish River. Midas bled to death. His *schmeckle* was heavy. It sunk to the bottom of the river. Marianna put Midas's body on a log and it floated downstream on the Swish River. His body was found in the town of *Brennholz* and his *schmeckle* was not found until several months later. A few boys were fishing and Midas's *schmeckle* got caught on one of the boy's fishing pole hook. He removed the *schmeckle* and put it into a basket that had been floating down the *Swish River.*

The police knew that Midas was a womanizer so they believed that a jealous husband killed Midas and cut off his *schmeckle.*

It was Bupkis regional news. Coincidentally, a basket retailer found the *schmeckle* under some wood chips in the basket He sent it to the Kishkapolis police. He had read about the murder in his local newspaper.

The police snapped a picture of the *schmeckle* and placed the picture on a flyer that they distributed around the town. It looked familiar to Marianna because there was a distinct tattoo on the tip. It was a dollar sign. She told no one!

His death remained a mystery to everyone in *Kishkapolis.* It became a cold case and remained that way.

CHAPTER XV

MELEK ZITSONTUSH
MOYSHE'S 2ND GREAT GRANDFATHER

Melek was an inventor. Melek had worked for his father Mendel. Melek discovered new methods to manufacture wallpaper. He was also a good businessman so he opened many small stores throughout *Kishkapolis* to sell his wallpaper products directly to end users.

Melek knew that he had to overcome the community residents' hatred toward Mendel and Midas. He had a different attitude than his father and brother. Melek knew that it was important to be well respected in the community. He used his wealth to establish shelters for the homeless. He gave gifts to many of the poor children and he lowered the rent for his tenants. Every year he invited his employees to join him for turkey dinner on the Mensche Holiday Hanukah and the Nudnik Holiday Christmas. He knew it was important for the community to flourish so he did everything in his power to help the town's business men succeed. Melek was wealthy enough to help many merchants pay their Business taxes. He never expected anything in return.

However, he was rewarded. His generosity was appreciated; thus, more people bought the wallpaper products from his small stores; the small stores that eventually became large stores. Melek was active in community organizations.

He founded the first *Kishkapolis* Boys Club. Teenagers 13-19 years old could join. Instructors taught them how to play indoor sports; ping pong, checkers and tidily winks. Instructors taught them outdoor sports; horse shoes, three-leg races and water balloon tosses. Several National tidily winks champions emerged from *Kishka*polis Boys Club.

Melek financially supported *Kishkapolis* Dandelions Organization which is similar to the Girls Scouts of America. The Dandelions learned crochet, knitting and sewing. Some of the best baby's clothes were made by the *Kishkapolis* Dandelions.

Kishkapolis citizens were seeking entertainment venues other than horseshoes, ping pong, tidily winks and checkers.

Melek sponsored chicken races for the local citizens to place bets. This was the forerunner of the more popular cow races. Pigeon flights were a popular sport sponsored by Melek. Heavy weights were placed on the pigeon's legs; bets were placed on the distance the pigeons could fly and then drop to the ground from pure exhaustion carrying the heavy weights. He sponsored canoe races that were held on the *Swish River*.

Melek led and paid for expeditions up the 250 feet *Sky High* Mountains. This kept the *Kishkapolis* explorers busy for four hours each time they climbed the mountain The citizens' of *Kishkapolis* were so appreciative of his generosity; they gave him a key to the city and honored him with "Melek Zitsontush Day". Until the day he died, Melek kept looking for the door that the key opened. He never found it and no one else knew which door it was.

There were many Zitsontush cousins so he organized a Zitsontush Cousins' Club. He wanted all of his cousins to stay in touch with each other. In honor of his father Mendel, he founded the Mendel Anti-Greed Association. This was his way of letting people know that he did not agree with his father's philosophy.

He hired well known national speakers to espouse the benefits of sharing and giving well being. The Greedy rich businessmen and financial leaders were not allowed to join the Anti-Greed Association. Melek and his wife Marianna had one son Herman.

CHAPTER XVI

HERMAN ZITSONTUSH (TUSHMAN) MOYSHE'S GREAT GRANDFATHER

Herman was Moyshe's Great Grandfather. He was slender and 6'4"tall; his attractive features and wealth made it impossible to keep the girls away. That didn't bother him at all.

Herman was very generous; a good trait that he learned from his father Melek. Herman did not desire to work in the Zitsontush family Company. The only company that he desired was the company of women, many women. He decided to learn a hobby to keep busy when he was not chasing women. Herman enjoyed working with his hands. He had plenty of experience using his hands when he dated women.

Herman and Yosef Bockermon were best friends when they met in college. Yosef worked for his own father. Mr. Bokerman owned a bakery in *Kishkapolis*.

Yosef and his father were always arguing. "You're putting too much sugar in the recipe. Sugar is expensive". That was one of Mr.

Bokerman's biggest complaints. "I'm following the recipe as you wrote it" retorted Yosef. Mr. Bokerman had other complaints.

"You're spilling flour all over the floor"

"Why can't you stir the ingredients faster?"

"It's 4:00 AM and you're still sweeping the floor. You should have been finished ten minutes ago and you are leaving dust on the floor".

Yosef shouted with frustration. "It's not my fault that the electric vacuum cleaner has not been invented yet!"

"You never praise me when I bake a good plain bagel with your recipe."

You never praised me when I created my own recipe to make marble rye bagels, poppy seed bagels, cinnamon-raison bagels and sesame seed bagels."

Mr. Bokerman continued to complain.

"You always forget to turn off the lights at night, Kerosene is very expensive." Moyshe's responses were made to closed ears. Mr. Bokerman continued to complain.

"Why didn't you go to the farm in rural *Kish* to buy eggs and milk for the strudel?"

"How can we make kishka without pigs' intestines?"

Yosef was finally fed up with his father. Although he loved his father, Yosef couldn't work for him.

Yosef decided to go to college to become an accountant. Herman asked his father Melek to give Yosef a job in the Zitsontush Family Company. Melek knew that Yosef was a bright man. Yosef could be trusted so Melek hired him. Yosef worked in the accounting department of the Company.

When Melek died Herman inherited the entire Zitsontush Family Company. He was 25 years old.

This is when Herman's story becomes most interesting.

Herman was too busy chasing women so he never learned how to run the Family Company and he did not want to learn.

Fortunately, his best friend Yosef had been working for the Zitsontush Family Company for several years and he understood how to run the Business. Most important, Yosef was a very honest man. Herman appointed Yosef to the position of Chief Financial Officer. Herman gave him complete control of the Business.

With Yosef running the Business, Herman was able to vacation and live the life of a playboy. That he did. He was a "skirt chaser". He tried to *shtoop* as many female *Nudniks* as he could. He did respect his parents' wish that he not *shtoop* any girls that belonged to the same *Mensche* Temple that he belonged. Yosef was concerned for Herman. He advised Herman on business and personal issues. He told Herman to stop chasing all of the female *Nudniks*. Yosef told Herman that the female *Nudniks* were gold diggers. He was spending too much money on expensive gifts and vacations for the female *Nudniks*. If Herman continued this life style he would go through his money faster than the *Swish River* flowed through the city of *Kishkapolis* and he would lose his Family Company. Herman knew that there was no way he could spend all of the money that he had. Although Herman was *Ongeshtopt mit gelt* (very wealthy), he listened intently to Yosef. He stopped chasing women but he still vacationed. He vacationed quite often. Herman knew that he had more money than he could spend in three lifetimes. Herman trusted Yosef He did not question Yosef's judgment. Yosef did well for Herman. He grew the Business even larger.

During a vacation, Herman met Chutzpah in her home town of Shpielkes. It was located in the resort community of Vorst in the country of Bupkis. Chutzpah was a slender woman with fine facial features. Her dark brown eyes, a tiny nose and high cheek bones were admired by many other women in Shpielkes. She was 5'1" tall.

They married and they decided to live in *Kishkapolis* on Best Avenue, the same street that the manufacturing factory was located. It was close enough for Herman to walk to work the one day of the week that he chose to work. The only reason that he went to work for the one day, which was actually only for two hours was to meet with Yosef to have a drink of *Kish* Merlot wine. They discussed Herman's escapades that week. This gave Yosef the opportunity to discuss the Business. The factory was closed on

Saturday, the seventh day of the week, It was the Sabbath, the day that Supreme Being rested after creating the world, according to the *Mensche* religion.

After two years of marriage, Chutzpah longed to return to her home town of Shpielkes. She never stopped complaining of her life in the big city of *Kishkapolis*. To please his wife whom he loved dearly, Herman sold his Company and they moved to Shpielkes. Herman rewarded Yosef because of his loyalty to him; he gave Yosef 25 percent of the profits from the sale of the Company. He gave 15 percent to his loyal factory workers. He donated 10 percent to the *Mensche* Temple and he kept 50 percent for himself. Herman was certainly not a *khazer*. He had more wealth than most men could dream about.

Herman was ecstatic that he was able to reward Yosef and his workers the portion of profits that they had earned. It was actually them that grew the Company. This made Yosef a very wealthy man. Although Herman lived in Shpielkes and Yosef lived in *Kishkapolis*, they continued their friendship.

Chutzpah, not an active woman, became fat with rose-colored cheeks that always appeared to be full of marbles. She was not satisfied with her life in Shpielkes. She was bored with very little to occupy her time. She was a selfish woman. She did not do any charity work. Chutzpah only knew how to complain to Herman and eat food. She ate a lot of food. No wonder she kept growing sideways. Nothing could satisfy this woman.

Herman was retired. He did not have to work after selling the wallpaper business. He did charity work and he hung wallpaper just to keep busy because at work he was able to find some relief from Chutzpah's constant nagging. At the end of each day, trying to relax by the wood burning fireplace, he could not escape her screeching voice. He thought to himself "OY VEY OY VEY" (WOE IS ME). He verbalized to her: "DU FARKIRTST VEY DI YORN" (YOU WILL BE THE DEATH OF ME). Herman vacationed often without Chutzpah.

He finally tired of listening to Chutzpah's complaints. Herman made a bold decision. They did not have any children so he packed his canvas bag, with only his own clothes and his entire life savings, which was plentiful. Chutzpah had no idea how much money Herman had accumulated. She had no money of her own.

Herman contacted his friend Yosef. Yosef never married. Herman told Yosef of his plans. They traveled to America. Herman left Chutzpah in Bupkis to fend for herself She continued to live in Shpielkes. Her parents were dead and she did not have any relatives or friends. Herman took all of the money that he had hidden in his home. The Bupkis banks were failing. He did not trust leaving his money in the banks. Herman assumed *that Chutzpah* would eventually marry a man that could support her and tolerate her nagging. He really didn't care!

Herman and Yosef boarded the Holland America steamship "Rotterdam" in Rotterdam, Netherlands.

As they were boarding the ship, Yosef heard the shrieking of a wild woman. He recognized the voice. Herman and Yosef recognized the voice.. Yosef looked back over his shoulder to watch the "crazy" lady that stood on the dock screaming profanities. She was flailing her arms haphazardly in the air. It was Chutzpah. She screamed *"Ayin Kafin Yan,* Shtick drek" (Go crap in the ocean, you piece of shit). Herman never looked back! Protective of Herman, Yosef shouted to Chutzpah" *Geh tren zikh "(Go* screw yourself). The ship left the dock. Although the ship was more than a thousand yards away, Herman and Yosef could hear her screaming. "Go *Puhtz* (dick head); *a Schmuck* (Prick) like you do not deserve me". He he thought to himself, "she was right. He deserved better!"

Within a few days the ship encountered the high rolling waives of the Atlantic Ocean. As the dark clouds loomed overhead, the heavy down pour of rain rocked the ship from side to side.

The ship was over crowded with immigrants standing shoulder to shoulder with no place to move. They were forced to live in the cargo area of the ship. The wealthy immigrants were also forced to live in the cargo area. They could not bribe the captain of the ship.

He left the rocking ship. The rolling motion of the ship made the captain seasick, He was not on the ship. He came to America in a hot air balloon. The sickness around Herman and the shortness of food and fresh water was one of the worse things that he had ever experienced, It fell just short of his miserable life with Chutzpah. His horrible experience on the sea was worth it. It was better than living with Chutzpah.

He did not have to see or hear from Chutzpah again. He could not let her know and she better never find out where he was settling in America.

Herman was not a stranger to chatting with women. He introduced himself to Arielle, a woman passenger on the ship. "*Gut morgn*" (good morning) my name is Herman Zitsontush". Arielle laughed out loud. He asked her if he could be in on the joke.

Arielle said "In English your name translates *to PIMPLES ON YOUR ASS*. You are a handsome man Herman Zitsontush. You will have no trouble attracting women. I recommend that you change your name to Herman Tushman; it means Ass Man. Women will admire your good looks and understand that you could very well be an "Ass Man". They will not laugh!

For the remainder of the trip Herman gave it some serious thought.

It was a long trip, the passengers, distraught from the voyage, disembarked on Ellis Island at the Port of New York City. There were thousands of immigrants crowded together like a pack of animals. They impatiently waited in long lines to enter America.

Herman walked down the ramp of the ship, He saw this scene of turmoil and he said to Yosef "*Oy Vey!*" Yosef responded. "I agree; what we have done?"

The Customs Agents were frustrated with the immigrants. Most of them could not speak English. The Agents hurried the immigrants through the lines. The immigrants had heavy European accents that the Agents found difficult to understand. The immigrants were just as frustrated. The immigrants couldn't understand the Agents. With a heavy *Mensche* accent, Moyshe's Great Grandfather Herman told the Custom Agent his name.

Herman Zitsontush decided that he would start anew in America. He said, "My name is Herman Tushman, The Ass Man". The Agent hastily wrote: Herman Tushman. He is not married. His trade is wallpaper hanger. Yosef was next in line. He told the Agent that his name was Yosef Bockermon. The Customs Agent wrote Yosef Bakerman. He is not married. His trade is baker.

Herman and Yosef had no idea of where to go or how to get there when they disembarked the ship.

A small group of immigrants gathered together to discuss their predicament. Fortunately, or not, a Port Authority Agent approached them and asked if he could be of help. One of the immigrants told him, in broken English that the Agent could hardly understand, of their predicament. The agent told the immigrants of a bustling city along side of a beautiful river. The city had a mild climate (it was summer time) and a wonderful opportunity to earn money in the grain mills.

Herman knew that he could hang wallpaper in any city and he was wealthy enough to retire, if he wanted. Yosef was capable of learning quickly He knew that he could learn anything. He decided that he would work in the grain mills. He was wealthy enough to retire, if he wanted!

What city in America could offer them more? Without hesitation, they traveled to Buffalo, New York.

Herman obtained a *"GET"* before leaving for America. A *"GET"* is a document that was approved by the Ibbar (*Mensche* Religious Leader) to dissolve a marriage. According to *Mensche* custom that freed him from Chutzpah, allowing him to marry another woman.

Herman met Gerta, a soft spoken, tall, slender, 5'9" brunette. She was nothing like Chutzpah. Already, Herman fell in love with her. Within three weeks they married. Herman and Gerta traveled all over America and Europe. Gerta wanted to see where Herman lived in Europe. They visited *Kishkapolis*. The factory building was torn down. They took the train from *Kishkapolis* to Shpielkes. That was a huge mistake!

Herman and Gerta were lying on the sandy beach of beautiful Lake *Aquah* that Herman vacationed often. They were sitting on a blanket looking toward the lake when Herman heard a familiar voice. It was a woman's voice; she shrieked "*Schmuck,* how dare you come back here?" What were the odds that Herman would cross paths with Chutzpah? He jumped up from the blanket, grabbed Gerta's hand and ran like hell! Herman was concerned that Chutzpah would follow, so he and Gerta cut their vacation in Europe short. They returned to America.

Herman and Gerta were very happily married. They had a son Morris.

Herman did not chase women in America as he did in Bupkis. Gerta volunteered at the local hospital in Buffalo. She played canasta and mahjong twice a week to keep herself busy.

Morris Tushman learned from his father Herman how how to hang wallpaper. Although Herman was retired, he hung wallpaper for a hobby. He never charged his family members and friends for his work.

Yosef had learned the bakery business when he worked for his father in *Kishkapolis.* He baked cookies, cakes, other desserts and the best challahs in Buffalo so he distributed them throughout New York State.

Challahs are made in various sizes and shapes, all of which have a meaning. Braided challahs have three, four, or six strands. They are the most common. They look like arms intertwined. They symbolize love. Three braids symbolize truth, peace, and justice. Twelve braids made from two small breads or one large braided bread recall the miracle of the 12 tribes of Bupkis. Round loaves have no beginning and no end. They are baked for Hanukah to symbolize continuity. They are served at the meal before the fast of Yom Ruppik.

Yosef believed that he was indebted to Herman for all of the wealth that Herman had given to him. Herman appreciated that

Yosef managed the Company in *Kishkapolis* for him and he would never forget that Yosef came to America. Herman did not need money so he would not accept any repayment from Yosef.

In honor of his good friend, Yosef named his best product *"Herman's Challahs"*.

Although Yosef was as wealthy as Herman, he did not retire in America. He became wealthier; he opened twenty "Herman's Challahs" locations. He was never married and he had no children to share his wealth. Yosef became ill; he did not sell his stores. He gave each store to the store's manager.

Herman died of a sudden heart attack. He did not suffer. Yosef, frail from his illness and distraught over his best friend's death, died one month later.

Herman's will was very specific. He wished to be fair to Gerta and Morris. He was unfair to Chutzpah. He really hated Chutzpah even though many years had passed. He donated one-half of his wealth to charity; one-fourth of his wealth was bequeathed to Gerta and one-fourth to his son Morris.

CHAPTER XVII

GRANDFATHER MORRIS TUSHMAN

Morris Tushman experienced the turn of the 20th
century.
In Europe, the Bristle Empire was as strong as
it ever had been in previous years.

Germland and Italand became unified nations in the second
half of the 20th century. They grew in power, challenging the
traditional power of Bristle and Francland. The European powers
competed with each other for land, military strength and economic
power.

Asia and Africa were for the most part still under control of
their European colonizers. The major exceptions were China and
Japan. The Russo-Japanese War in 1904-1905 was the first major
instance of a European power being defeated by a so-called inferior
nation

America was emerging as an industrial power as well, rivaling
Bristle, Germland, and Francland.

With increasing rivalry among the European powers and the
rise of Japan and the United States, the stage was set for a major
upheaval in world affairs.

The Wright brothers invented the airplane in 1903. The First Bupkis War, termed "The Great War" (or simply BWI) by contemporaries, started in 1914 and ended in 1918. Morris enlisted and fought in Bupkis War I. He said that he was 18 years old although he was only 17 years old; he entered as a Private and ended his service as a Private. He was not a coward; he had no ambition to advance rank. He did not kill any enemy; he did not save any lives. He just wanted to get back alive to his family in the United States.

Communism was strengthened as a force in Western democracies when the global economy crashed in 1929 in what became known as the Great Depression.

There was also a strong appeal to a mythical racial purity (the idea that Germlands were the "master race") and vicious anti-*Mensche* which promoted the idea of *Mensche* as trouble makers. Anti-*Mensche* during the Great Depression was rampant because many people were content to blame the *Mensche* for causing the economic downturn

Morris Tushman was an avid supporter of *Mensche*, Zionism and a proponent of American Socialism. Zionism was a world-wide movement that resulted in the establishment and development of the state of Israel. Morris donated most of his wealth to Zionism and *Mensche* movement. Although his donations were generous, he and Zofia lived a comfortable life and he bequeathed a small fortune to his son Michael.

After the Great Depression, Morris continued to keep on top of current affairs; he was concerned about the economy so he decided to hang wallpaper in case the balance of his investments decreased in value.

He and Zofia moved to Los Angeles, California. He had an offer from a large movie studio to hang wallpaper to be used as backdrops for movie scenes. Morris earned a substantial living. He met many famous and wealthy moguls in the movie industry. The movie industry was growing. The first talking movie was produced. There were more paper hanging jobs than Morris could handle. He did not want to disappoint the movie moguls that he met in the movie industry so he hired a crew to take over the paper hanging jobs. The moguls were thankful to Morris for his referrals. Morris and Zofia missed their friends so they moved back to Buffalo. Morris knew how to hang wallpaper; that's what he knew best.

He should have continued to do what he knew best. Morris remembered stories about his 4th Great Grandfather Mazel. He owned the Silver and Gold Mines in the *Sky High* Mountains that he inherited from his brother-in-law Goldan Mann. Mazel was very successful with the silver and gold mines. Morris did not consider that the mines were producing gold and silver before Mazel owned them.

Morris had a good friend Irving Gunman. Irving was Morris's stock broker. He told Morris about "Rising Silver Mines" in Arizona; "RSM" on the Stock Exchange. It was a penny stock that could be bought for 32 cents. Morris bought 500,000 shares. The stock cost him $160,000; 90% of his life savings. It was a wise purchase, the stock doubled in one month. Morris deposited $320,000 in an escrow account to be used for future investments.

Irving invested $100,000 in "Rising Gold Mines" and recommended that Morris do the same. There was an article in the Wall Street News that gold had been discovered in the "Rising Gold Mines" Morris doubled his money in the first investment that Irving recommended. So he was confident that he would profit again.

Morris was positive that he was as smart as Mazel so he invested $300,000 in the gold stock. He didn't realize two things: first, Mazel was a lucky man. Second, He did not read the entire article; it was "Fool's Gold" that was discovered. Morris lost all of his money. Zofia screamed "Oy Vey!" She told Morris to do what he knew best; hang wallpaper. He was not a *Puhtz* so he paid good attention to Zofia. He called the movie moguls in Los Angeles and asked them if they had any wallpaper hanging jobs for him.

They were very polite when they told Morris that he was a *schmuck* (stupid man). The crew that Morris had referred was doing a very competent job and they were not going to change paperhangers. Morris was more like his 4ᵗʰ Great Uncle Schlemiel than his 4ᵗʰ Great Grandfather Mazel. He had no luck. Zofia told him that they were going to live in Buffalo and he was going to continue hanging wallpaper to support his pregnant wife. They had one son Michael Tushman.

MICHAEL TUSHMAN
MOYSHE'S FATHER

Moyshe's father Michael worked for his father Morris when he was 14 years old. He pasted wallpaper while his father hung it. Morris was not satisfied with Michael's pasting abilities so he "fired" him. Morris saved 45 cents an hour now that he didn't have to pay Michael.

Michael was pissed! He decided to run away from his home in Buffalo at the young age of 14 years old. He had $3 in his pocket and the clothes that he was wearing.

Michael walked from his home on Winslow Street to the Train Station on Paderewski Street. When the train conductor was not looking he hopped into one of the box cars. He heard squealing noises. The hogs were eating hay that was scattered across the floor. There were three unshaven, unkempt men sitting on the left side toward the back of the box car. They were smoking cigarettes and drinking Thunderbird wine straight from the dark green color pint bottle.

Michael moved to the right side. The train started to roll and he was on his way west to Los Angeles. It was pitch black inside the box car. He thought about the sites that he would see. The first stop would be St. Louis, Missouri; the famous Gateway Arch to the west should be interesting. Michael lay down his head on a small stack of hay, closed his eyes and fell asleep. The train came to a screeching halt. Morris heard the sound of a whistle as the box car door opened. A uniformed man with a flashlight looked inside and screamed "get out". The three men and Michael jumped to their feet and ran out of the box car, shoving the uniformed man to the ground.

Michael separated from the three men and he continued to run. He assumed that the towering Archway would be visible from the St. Louis Train Station. It was nowhere in sight. He walked into the depot building to find a rest room.

Michael read the sign that was inside the doorway to the building: "WELCOME TO ALBANY, NEW YORK". He couldn't believe it; he hopped on a train that went east, not west.

Michael had 50 cents left in his pocket. He had spent $2.50 on peanuts, popcorn and cracker jacks before he left Buffalo. He found a pay phone; put 10 cents into the slot and dialed "0" (operator"). He crossed his fingers and prayed that his father Morris or mother Zofia would accept a collect call. The operator hung up the phone when Morris declined the call. The dime was in the return slot. Michael redialed "0" and told the operator that he wanted to make a collect call, person to person to Zofia Tushman. Michael peed in his pants awaiting her response. She accepted the call and he began to sob incessantly. He asked his mother to forgive him for running away.

Zofia said that Michael had to ask his father for forgiveness, not her. Morris got on the phone. Michael begged for forgiveness. Morris accepted his apology on one condition: Michael could return home but he would have to paste wallpaper for him. Michael accepted! He had two problems. His father did not offer to send him money and he only had 40 cents left in his pocket. He sobbed silently to himself "Oy Vey Oy Vey". He could not afford to buy any popcorn, peanuts or cracker jacks. Worse than that, he had to find a train going west back to Buffalo. He prayed that he didn't have to hop in to a box car loaded with hogs. His prayers were answered! The box car loaded with hogs passed by him. He hopped into a box car loaded with chickens. He arrived home. His mother and father greeted him with open arms. Zofia's open arms gave him a big hug. His father's open arms grabbed him by the neck as he told Michael to go to his room because he would have to get up at 7:00 AM to paste wallpaper the next morning. Michael obeyed!

Michael worked for Morris approximately two years. He did not run away from home; he quit working for Morris

He borrowed money from his Uncle Alan to start a business at the age of 16 years old. He opened a ping pong and pool hall business on Main Street in Buffalo. His customers smoked cigars and burnt holes in the velvet tops of the pool tables. They hit the ping pong balls too hard causing them to form dents or they lost their balls. That lasted 6 months! His uncle agreed to forgive the debt with the understanding that Michael would paste wallpaper for him.

Alan and Morris were competitors. Morris refused to allow Michael to work for Alan. Michael, with his *schmeckle* between his legs, pasted wallpaper for his father Morris. That lasted two years. Michael made enough money to pay the debt to his Uncle Alan. Michael was 18 years old when he borrowed money from his Uncle Thomas to start his own business hanging wallpaper.

Morris permanently injured his leg when he fell from a tree on a Sunday trying to rescue his neighbor's pet cat. Michael did not hold a grudge against his father so he offered him a job. Morris could not climb a ladder because of his injured leg so he pasted wallpaper for Michael.

Michael met and married Moyshe's mother Michelle (née Leifver) in 1940. They had three children, Barney, Moyshe and Marissa. Barney was born in 1941; Moyshe was born in 1944; Marissa was born in 1947.

MOYSHE'S MISSION TO BECOME A FOUNTAIN PEN

CHAPTER I

MOYSHE THE ELEMENTARY SCHOOL STUDENT

Moyshe is a fourth generation American *Mensche,* born in Buffalo, New York.

September 1949, the day after Labor Day, Moyshe began kindergarten, his very first day of school.

He wore a white T-shirt under his red and black plaid long sleeve wool shirt with cream color plastic buttons. The white T-shirt prevented the wool shirt from scratching his large frame body. The size 34 husky, brown, lined corduroy wool pants fit tightly on his ass and thick legs. He wore tightie-whities under his brown corduroy pants. Moyshe did not wear a diaper because he was five years old; he stopped pooping in his pants when he was four years old. Heavy brown wool socks matched his pants and brown, wide-toe Buster Brown shoes.

Barney told Moyshe that Buster Brown's dog "Tide" lived in the shoe and it would bite him if he stepped on him too hard. "Tide's" picture was imprinted on a white sticker that was mounted toward the back of the shoe so Moyshe walked on his toes quite often because he didn't want to hurt "Tide".

Michelle wet her fingers with her tongue to smooth down the little dab of Brylcreme that made his hair shiny black. His hair was parted in the middle of his head. Yuk!

His father was working, hanging wallpaper so his mother walked the three short blocks to School #81.His Brother Barney walked with them. Bubby stayed home with his sister Marissa. She was too young to attend school.

As they approached school there were two long lines formed with boys standing on the right and girls standing on the left. There were two entrances to the school. Above the wide doorway on the left there was a sign "GIRLS" engraved into a concrete block; "BOYS" was engraved into the concrete block above the wide doorway on the right side.

A bell rang. All students "slowly" rushed into school. Moyshe looked back over his shoulder. His mother waved to him; tears started to swell in her dark brown eyes and began to gush down her cheeks. She tried to hide her tears; she didn't want Moyshe to cry. He didn't cry; he couldn't have been happier.

Moyshe's Kindergarten teacher was old, short and fat. She looked like a barrel, not made of wood. Her unkempt mousy brown hair was pulled back on the sides with a small short pony tail on the back of her head. Although she looked old, she was probably only twenty-five years old! Her name "Miss Logan" was written in white chalk on the blackboard. Moyshe thought that it was strange that her name was written on the board. The children were only five years old, they could not read! The class consisted of 15 girls and 15 boys.

There was a long dark gray metal cabinet along the back wall of the room. Miss Logan assigned an open cubicle to each of them. Each cubicle was divided into two sections; a small shelf on the top, a hook below the shelf and a tall open space below the top shelf. She told the children to put their heavy braided gray and black wool floor mats below. Coats were to be hung on the hook if they had a coat. Everyone's floor mat was the same color black and gray. Moyshe don't know why they were all black and gray. Black and gray were certainly not the school colors. In fact, he didn't believe that there were school colors.

The school bell rang and class begun. The students sat in a circle as Miss Logan read a story to them; it was about three bears that ate porridge, a girl with gold color hair ate the baby bear's porridge, broke the baby bear's chair and slept in the baby bear's bed. That was ridiculous! Moyshe knew that bears did not eat porridge.

Miss Logan finished the story; she looked at the large round clock mounted on the wall. It was not digital; it had large black Roman numeral numbers written around the circumference. She told the children that it was time for rest period. They went to the cubicles to get their mats. The children formed two lines of mats on the floor.

Moyshe took off his shoes, socks, plaid shirt, T -shirt and corduroy pants. He was the only one standing in his tightie whities with nothing else on his body. Miss Logan looked directly at him. Her face was redder than a red grape. She was screaming like a "wild banshee as she scolded Moyshe "It's disgusting that you are standing in your tightie-whities" Moyshe was confused. He cried and whimpered. "Doesn't everyone get undressed to take a nap?" Perhaps he should have kept the socks on his feet!

The boys laid on the mats to the right, the girls on the mats to the left. Why were boys always on the right and the girls on the left? What would happen if they did not know whether they were a boy or a girl? It did not take Moyshe long to figure it out. There certainly was a big difference between girls and boys. Girls had long hair and wore a skirt or dress. Boys had short hair and wore long brown lined corduroy pants and brown wide toe Buster Brown shoes with his dog Tide in there too.

Miss Logan never stopped scolding Moyshe, especially during nap time because he continually looked up the girls' dresses when they were lying on their mats. Moyshe asked himself, "Wasn't that normal?" Every day Miss Logan sighed with relief when nap time was over.

She handed out crayons and paper; the children drew pictures of their family. He drew a picture of two really fat children, Barney and Marissa; they really weren't fat. He drew a picture of his thin mother, father, Bubby and himself. The dog had four legs, two huge ears and a long tongue hanging out of its mouth even though they didn't own a dog; so he drew a picture that resembled "Tide", Buster Brown's dog. The school bell rang and class was over. Michelle picked him up from school. He only attended half day. His mother Michelle and he walked home. Barney remained in school. He walked home with his friends when his classes ended; three hours later.

Michelle asked Moyshe about his first day; "What did you do in school?"

Moyshe told her "Miss Logan read us a boring story about the three bears and the girl with golden color hair." Michelle exclaimed "that was wonderful!" He didn't tell her that he was bored because Bubby already told him that story.

Moyshe told her about rest period; that he could see up the girls' dresses when they were lying on their mats. She exclaimed "that was not wonderful!"

He told her that Miss Logan was nasty; she screamed at him for getting undressed during rest period. Michelle exclaimed "that is not wonderful!" He wasn't sure whether his mother was upset that Miss Logan screamed at him or that he undressed for rest period. He was confused!

September 1950 the day after Labor Day, he advanced to first grade. He knew that he would advance. Bubby always told him that he was smart! It took the entire ten months of the school year for his class mates to learn the alphabet. It took him only 8 months. Moyshe was maturing rapidly so he was able to tell his stories in his own words.

I am maturing rapidly so here are my stories in my own words. September 1951 the day after Labor Day, I advanced to second grade. I learned how to read "See Dick run, See Jane run, and See Spot jump." I wondered why we didn't "See Buster Brown's dog Tide jump".

September 1952 the day after Labor Day, I advanced to third grade. I learned how to print with a number two black lead pencil. I printed perfect. I kept my numbers and letters within the wide lines on the rough off white color paper.

September 1953 the day after Labor Day I advanced to fourth grade. I learned how to draw a continuous round circle that was not supposed to end. The object was to not let the lines of one circle overlap the lines of another circle. I wasn't very good drawing those circles. I learned cursive and I learned how to write with ink instead of a number 2 pencil. My teacher Miss Jones handed me a 12" long wood stick, thin and pointed at one end; thick and round at the other end. There was a semi circle carved into the surface of the round end. A pointed metal object was placed into the semi circle. She handed me a bottle of blue ink that I placed into a round hole in the upper right corner of my light brown wood desk. I dipped the point of the metal object into the ink bottle. The ink rose up into the slit in the metal point.

I wrote my name on a piece of paper. It was messy! There were blotches of ink on the paper, on the desk and on my hands. It took three days of scrubbing to get my hands completely clean. It never came off of the desk. I learned how to write my name on the desk and scratch my name into the top of my desk using a heavy metal paper clip. I guess I wasn't supposed to do that!

My mother allowed me to walk home from school with my friends. We ate lunch at home because there was no cafeteria in school. After school I played with the same four friends. Neither one of us had become a fountain pen yet but we still shared stories about girls. I lied and exaggerated because I had never spoken to a girl except during rest period when I was in kindergarten. Perhaps I would know more if I took a net into the woods behind school and caught some birds and bees. I assumed that my friends lied also.

CHAPTER II

FOUR MENSCHE & ONE NUDNIK

My four friends and I were neighbors. We became best friends when we were in the same class room in fourth grade at School 81. We lived in North Buffalo on Commonwealth Avenue.

The neighborhood consisted of mostly *Mensche* and *Nudnik* families that were born in Bupkis and came to America to live on gold lined concrete streets. They were not smart enough to know that there were no pots of gold at the end of the rainbow because the leprechauns stayed in Ireland.

My "inner circle" of four friends and me did everything together. Four of us were *Mensche*; we did not believe that we were superior but we really believed that we were the "chosen" people. We weren't sure what that meant. It had to be true. Bubby told me so! Perhaps we would be chosen first to be on any sports team. Jacob, Saul, Richard and I were the "chosen ones; Richard hated to be called "Dick". Of course, we did call him Dick. In case I haven't mentioned, my name is Moyshe. The fifth member of our group was Frankie, our token Nudnik. He was a few years older but we were in the same class because he failed kindergarten twice. We needed him as a friend because as we grew older; he was the only one in our group that had a driver's license and a car.

Frankie said that he was an Atheist; that didn't matter. I believe that he was more confused than we were because he used to say "thank Supreme Being that I am an Atheist". He could have been any nationality or religion; as long as he wasn't a *Mensche*. If he was a *Mensche*, he couldn't be our token Nudnik. The four of us taught Frankie an important *Mensche* phrase *"Ess drek und shaarbin"*. We told him that it meant "Eat food and enjoy your meal". Every time we entered a restaurant and walked toward our table he said to the other restaurant patrons *"ess drek und shaarbin"* It actually meant "Eat shit and die"! We don't believe that he ever found out the true meaning and we don't believe that he even cared.

Frankie had sleek, greasy, ebony black color hair combed backward to form a D.A. (Duck's Ass) in the back of his head. He probably used more than one dab of Brylcreme! His well-sculpted body was proof that he lifted weights and maintained a strict diet of chicken for protein and vegetables as a side dish. I'm sure that he did not eat *kishka*. He was the tallest of our group.

Richard had a Buzz cut; it was difficult to determine the color of his hair. It was either very light red or light blonde. He was an inch shorter than Frankie. However, he was thinner.

Saul was shorter than Richard; his sandy brown color hair was never combed and probably never washed. He was chubby and he appeared to have a distinct, awful odor on his body at all times. We poked fun at him, just short of bullying. He was the shortest of our group.

Jacob was approximately the same height as Frankie, about ¼" shorter. Richard and I were the same height. Richard's well groomed dark blonde color hair was longer than Frankie's. He did not have a D.A. He was much more slender than Saul. However, he had handle bars that slightly protruded on the sides of his waist.

I was approximately the same height and weight as Richard; my dark black color hair was short and well groomed with a part on the left side. Hygiene was very important to me. I used my father's

Old Spice deodorant and cologne after my daily shower. I brushed my teeth with *Colgate* tooth paste immediately upon waking up in the morning; after every meal and before I went to sleep. Bubby insisted!

For entertainment we chased girls to keep ourselves busy when we weren't flipping or pitching trading cards. I remember one winter, we chased Rosemary; the Nudnik shiksal (non *Mensche* girl) that lived next door to me on Commonwealth Avenue. Our "*Mission*" was to run after her and "trap" her with a butterfly net. Frankie told us that it was the thing to do because she enjoyed it. I questioned Frankie; "if she enjoyed it why did she always run away?" We kept chasing! When my parents found out what we were doing, they grounded me for one month. I kept getting grounded for one month, four times because Frankie convinced me to continue chasing the girls and catching them with my butterfly net. It was a wide net so I was the most successful catcher.

Frankie told me that he "stole" some cigarettes from his mother's underwear drawer; that's where she hid them. We went into my garage to learn how to smoke. Jacob, Saul, Richard and I got sick. Frankie laughed, he didn't get sick.

I walked into my house; my face was a yellow-green color, my breath smelled of smoke and I was nervous.

My mother was standing at the door on the driveway side of our house. She saw smoke coming from the garage. Luckily for me, she did not dial 911. Unluckily for me, she saw the smoke signals. I entered the house and she asked me if I had been smoking.

I peed in my pants because I knew that I had to tell the truth. She didn't scold me. I wondered why she had a wide grin on her face. I had a feeling that a storm was a brewing! My father came home from work early. Barney and Marissa were giggling because they thought that I would be severely punished. My father told Barney and Marissa to leave the living room. He wanted to talk with me privately. I stood in the living room; that's the room where we received our punishment. I saw the steam rise from my father's eyes. I peed in my pants again. My father didn't say a word.

My mother said that she had been waiting all day to say something to me. She told me that she and my father had discussed my punishment. I knew I wasn't going to be grounded for one month. I would probably be grounded until I got married.

My father loosened his belt and told my mother that it was too tight around his waist. He had eaten too much for dinner. He did not take the belt off his pants. My mother handed me a pack of cigarettes and told me that I had to smoke all 32 cigarettes in front of them. Then I would have to smoke another pack of cigarettes in front of them.

I had not forgotten how sick I was from the three puffs that I had taken that afternoon in the garage. I never smoked again, for my entire life!

Commonwealth Avenue and Crestwood Avenue were two streets that ran parallel and adjacent to each other, separated only by the back sides of garages. The garages were detached from the houses. They were behind the houses of both streets. The garages were approximately three to four feet apart from each other.

Frankie dared us to jump from one garage to the other. No one ever got hurt because Saul, Jacob, Richard and I never accepted the dare.

There was an empty lot between two houses on Crestwood Avenue. We played tackle football. We did not wear helmets, padding or uniforms. No one ever tried to tackle Saul; he was too chubby and too smelly. We did convince Frankie, our token Nudnik to tackle Saul. He did it once. He hurt his head and it took four hours to wash the smell off his hands.

We used the empty lot that was between two houses on Commonwealth Avenue as a baseball field. We broke three windows the first day. I broke two of those three windows.

When I told my mother that I broke the windows she did not scold me. That evening my father came home early. He handed me two packs of cigarettes and told me that I could not play ball on those lots or I would know what I would have to do. I looked at the cigarettes; I remembered how sick I had gotten from the three puffs; I never played ball on that lot again.

There was a tall oak tree on the lot on Commonwealth Avenue. Everyone in the neighborhood, including boys and girls, climbed that tree. I stood on the ground with my hands cuffed together to help the girls reach the first branch of the tree. I let the boys fend for themselves. I enjoyed watching the girls climb; I could see their white panties when I gazed up their dresses. I let the girls that wore long pants fend for themselves! No one ever climbed above the first branch except Frankie, our token Nudnik Everyone fell off the tree at one time or another; Everyone except Frankie and my little sister Marissa.

Frankie lived next door to us. His driveway was on the same side as our kitchen window. He drove forward and backward in the driveway. My mother always screamed at him to stop or she would tell his father. Frankie did not have a driver's license. He was only 14 years old! His father didn't care that he drove forward and backward in the driveway.

Frankie's little brother Louie was 8 years old. He wet his pants quite often because he waited too long to go inside his house to use the toilet Sometimes he dropped his pants and crapped on the sidewalk. My brother Barney wondered why Louie's mother didn't carry a plastic baggie to clean the crap from the sidewalk.

On a warm summer day the flies swarmed around the crap and Frankie's dog *Stupid* used to sniff and pee on the crap. My mother always screamed that she was going to tell Frankie's father. His father didn't care that Louie crapped on the sidewalk.

I wore boots before I jumped on the crap to smooth it.

CHAPTER III

THE OSKOWITZ TWINS

It was 1953, I fell "in love" with the twins, Jackie and Judy Oskowitz. In my mind, they were the prettiest girls in the entire school, including the fifth to eighth graders. I never tried to catch them with a butterfly net because I didn't want them to get upset with me.

They lived on Lovering Avenue, one block closer to school than Commonwealth Avenue. I begged them to walk to school with me. I begged every day until they agreed. I would walk alone the one block to their house to meet with them. I held their hands as I walked between them. Jackie was always on the left side and Judy was on my right side.

I was the envy of every boy on Lovering Avenue and Commonwealth Avenue. Some of their fathers were envious of me also.

Jim Bronsosky "loved" them as much as I did. The twins were not aware of his "love" for them. He was too shy to tell them. Jim was jealous of me. He asked me if he could walk with us to school. I said "absolutely not". I did not like Jim; he was a bully.

Baron Z. Halpern

He wanted to fight with me because I refused to let him walk with us. Jim weighed twenty pounds more than me; I was sure that I could not beat him up; but I could beat him in a race.

I told him that I would not fight; then I pushed him into the school fence. His nose began to bleed; I ran like hell! He knew that he could not catch me, so he didn't chase.

Jim yelled that some day he would get even. I was afraid of him so every time I saw him walk toward me, I ran to the other side of the street. This continued only for six months because lucky for me, he and his family moved to Erie, Pennsylvania so I never saw him again. The twins never knew that Jim wanted to walk with us to school and I didn't tell them.

A school mate, Marty Robstrin lived on Crestwood Avenue one block further from school than Commonwealth Avenue. He asked the twins and me to go on a "double date". He wanted to take Judy; I agreed to take Jackie on the date. Marty walked to my house and we walked together to the twin's house.

The four of us walked three blocks to Vito's Pizzeria on Virgil Avenue at the corner of Tacoma Avenue. The girls did not know that we were pairing up. They were happy that the four of us went as friends. Marty and I paid for the pizza, the twins paid for the drinks. We didn't know enough to leave a tip. Jackie was wearing a white blouse that was loose around her upper right arm. I kept trying to sneak a peek. I think that she caught me a few times; however she never said a word to me about it. I kept dropping my silverware so that I could sneak a peek up their red and white skirts. They always wore matching outfits to confuse everyone about their identities, especially the teachers. After our "date" the four of us walked home; I held Jackie's hand, Marty held Judy's hand. I was walking on cloud nine. The twins were walking on the sidewalk. That day was one of the best times that I had ever experienced in all of my five years in Elementary School. Although we didn't even kiss on the cheek, it was probably better than sex! What did I know?

Jackie and Judy did not compete with each other in sports, school grades or boys.

The same evening of that "date" I remember there was a special event on television.

I invited the twins, Marty, Frankie and his brother Louie to watch the coronation of Queen Elizabeth II of England. We watched it on the black and white 14" screen Motorola TV in my living room. Frankie did not have a TV.

I was very impressionable. Although it was broadcast in black and white, I could imagine the colorful uniforms, flowers, dresses, etc,

The Coronation ceremony was held in Westminster Abbey. The route started at Buckingham Palace and ended at Westminster Abbey. The route was lined on both sides with military men and women. There was a procession that included foreign royalty and heads of state riding in various carriages. They moved along the promenade. The sidewalks were crowded with flag-waving people.

Queen Elizabeth II was sitting tall in her white gold plated carriage that was pulled by eight white horses. The Prime Minister of England sat atop a beautiful black horse that led the procession.

The TV coverage was so good that I could see the horses take a crap on the street.

It was a mistake to invite Louie. My mother was in the kitchen and she came into the living room. She screamed as loud as I have ever heard her scream, "WHAT ARE YOU DOING, GET OUT OF MY HOUSE!" I couldn't believe that she would get upset that we were watching TV.

I began to smell something; I looked at the floor in front of the TV. Frankie laughed and said "Louie must have seen the horses take a crap on TV. His pants were off. He had crapped in front of the TV." No wonder my mother screamed. That is what I remembered.

It was a very interesting and important historical event, but nothing could outshine my pizza date with the twins and Marty.

CHAPTER IV

MOYSHE THE ATHLETE

September 1954 the day after Labor Day, I advanced to fifth grade. I was on the baseball and basketball "C" team. I wasn't good enough to make the "A" or "B" team. My position was "catcher" on the baseball team. I was afraid of the large soft ball that the pitcher threw in a slow high arc toward home plate. I hoped that the batter would hit the ball so that I wouldn't have to try to catch it. If the batter swung and missed the ball, I closed my eyes, backed up and moved to the left. I never caught the ball; the back stop was not far behind me so I didn't have to jog too far to retrieve the ball.

I threw worse than I caught. I never reached the pitcher or I threw it over his head after I retrieved the ball. Mr. Johnston, the gym teacher always blamed me if the game took longer than it should have taken.

The playground was covered with crushed stone. That didn't stop us from sliding into second base, third base or home plate. At least, we could overrun first base so we didn't have to slide. I tore my long brown lined corduroy pants quite often sliding into second base. I was always tagged out because I ran too slowly to beat the ball thrown by the catcher to the second baseman. My mother never understood why I always tore my pants.

During the very first baseball game that we played I slid into second base, was tagged out, tore my pants and scraped my hands on the stone filled playground. I was dirty from head to toe. My hands were as bloody as they were dirty. Mister Johnson, the gym teacher told me to go into the locker room to wash my hands.

I was too lazy to walk all the way to the back of the locker room where the sinks were located. So, I washed them in the drinking fountain located in the front of the locker room. Mr. Johnson saw me washing my hands in the water fountain. He scolded me and sent me to the principal's office. The office walls were painted a dark cream color and the woodwork was a dark brown color. The high frosted glass windows were covered with cream plastic shades that were turning brown from aging. The Principal, Miss Olivia Garden wore thick eye glasses. She was as blind as a bat! The tops of the wide black color eye glass frames were always hanging below her eyebrows. The end of her wide nose prevented her eyeglasses from falling off her face. There was one time that I saw the eyeglasses fall off her face, bounce into her unbuttoned blouse and land into the cleavage of her long flabby boobs.

The punishment for misbehaving in class was the same as the punishment by Mr. Johnson. I had to sit in Miss Garden's office for one-half hour with my hands folded. I had nothing to do so I watched her walk back and forth across the room; her *tush* and *titsies* swinging in the air like a gorilla's arms, chest and ass.

One day our school basketball team was losing to our rivals, School #66. That was normal; we always lost to them.

We were behind by one point with eight seconds left in the game. I had the ball. It was my chance to be a hero. The coach Mr. Johnson would be proud of me if I could sink a basket to win the game. I took a shot from half court and it went into the basket. The game was over. We won the game, our first win ever over our arch rivals.

Mr. Johnson ran onto the court; I couldn't wait to be lifted by him to celebrate our victory. He grabbed me by the back of my neck and yanked me off the court. He scolded me for taking a shot from half court. He did not care that we won. He said that he was going to teach me a lesson. I knew that the season was over and there was nothing that he could do to punish me. However, there was one thing that he could do. He sent me to Miss Garden's office.

September 1956 the day after Labor Day, I advanced to sixth grade. I was looking forward to advancing from the "C" team to the "A" or "B" team in basketball and baseball. Mr. Owens was the gym teacher and coach of the sports teams. Everyone was looking forward to playing basketball and baseball for Mr. Owens; especially me! The basketball season was going to start in October and baseball was going to start in April. We couldn't believe it; Mr. Owens had a heart attack in late September; he died; Mr. Johnson took over Mr. Owens' responsibilities. My goose was cooked! Mr. Johnson took me to the side and said "LET BYGONES BE BYGONES".

He told me that I could play on the school teams if I was capable of joining the monkey club. I had no idea what he was talking about.

There were two heavy braided ropes hanging from the ceiling of the gym. Mr. Johnson forced me to climb the rope to reach a flag tied to the top of the rope. During the school season Mr. Johnson held contests. His contests consisted of one boy racing against the other on the ropes that were only three feet apart from each other. The winner of each race would have the "honor" to join the "monkey club" and the "honor" to be in the next race. The final winner was determined by process of elimination. The winner of the final competition would be declared "King Kong". No one, except Frankie wanted to be "King Kong".

Mr. Johnson believed that everyone wanted to join the monkey club. I never made it to the top. Mr. Johnson was a real *Puhtz!* He did not allow me to play on the 6th grade school basketball or baseball team.

Music class was less fun than gym class and I hated gym class. Every student was required to be in the school choir and learn to play an instrument. I chose the xylophone; all of the other instruments looked too difficult to play. I never conquered the xylophone. Miss Schvantz placed me in the last row of the choir and told me to mouth words; not to sing. I would never get the lead role in a musical!

CHAPTER V

JUNIOR HIGH SCHOOL

In January 1957, my parents decided to buy a bigger house so we moved to Allenhurst Road in the suburbs. The single family homes in the suburbs were mostly constructed of brick as opposed to the two family homes located in North Buffalo constructed of brown horizontal wooden slats. I was in seventh grade and I was distraught that the twins and I would not be attending the same school. Frankie. Richard and I made a pact to remain as friends and get together whenever possible.

I made new friends, boys and girls. It wasn't the same friendship that I had with my friends on Commonwealth Avenue but I was able to accept the new situation because Bubby said that things would get better for me. At first, I did feel very strange because we lived in a neighborhood with a majority of Nudniks and very few Mensche. There was no bus service from Commonwealth Avenue to School 81; there were only three blocks separating them. There was no bus service from Allenhurst Road to Junior High School; they were 8 miles apart from each other. My three friends Patrick, Darby, Arvin and I hitch hiked to school every morning. A nice looking young lady that picked us up was real kind. She must have been approximately 35 years old. Her name was Betsy. She drove an English *Morris Minor* automobile. Betsy drove us to school many times. We had to squeeze shoulder to shoulder to fit inside.

One morning my friends were sick so I was alone. Betsy stopped her car, opened the door and winked as she told me to sit next to her on the front seat.

I thought that she spoke a lot of nonsense. She said that she was glad that I was alone. I didn't mind. Betsy was an elementary school teacher. It was a cold winter morning and she asked me to reach in to the back seat and get a brown and yellow crocheted afghan. We arrived to the front of school but she didn't stop.

A few miles down the road we came to a small one way street and she took a right hand turn. It was a dead end street secluded among trees, not houses. At the end of the street, Betsy parked the car and put the afghan over our laps. Upon her command, I opened the glove compartment and she reached in.

I had some concern on my mind. Was she reaching in for a gun? Would I never see my parents again? She told me to release the lever on the side of my seat and let the back of the seat recline; close my eyes and relax. I followed her instructions. I was relaxed with my hands cupped on the top of my head. It was exciting when she unzipped my jeans. Then I felt something cold on my *schmeckle*. I opened my eyes; it was a gun. I panicked, so I opened the car door and I jumped out of the car and slipped on a patch of ice. I was lying on my back; she stuck her hand out the door and I saw her pull on the trigger. Nothing happened so the gun must have jammed. I got up and ran like hell. I heard a loud sound; similar to a gun shot. I did not fall to the ground so I know that she missed me. As I ran faster, I looked back over my shoulder. I saw that she was still holding the gun. However, there was a Bupkis flag hanging from the barrel of the gun. She laughed out loud as she screamed "come back, it's a trick gun".

I thought to myself "this lady is crazy, perhaps she has a knife". I held my *schmeckle* tight as I kept running away from her.

I never told my friends what happened. I was too embarrassed. My friends couldn't understand why she kept driving by us and she never picked us up for school again.

After school we played baseball pick-up games. There were no organized sports leagues in Junior High School. Patrick, Darby, Arvin and I were playing sandlot baseball with a bunch of fellows. Our team was losing 4-3 in the bottom of the ninth. We were the home team, bases were loaded, there were two outs and I was at bat. All year I never got a hit. All I had to do was walk, hit a single or get hit by a pitch to get on base and we would tie the game.

The first pitch came across the plate, I swung and missed. The next two pitches were a ball and the next pitch was a perfect strike but I did not swing. The count was three balls and two strikes. This was the last pitch of the game; I followed the ball as it left the pitcher's hand toward me and straight across the plate.

I took a perfect swing at the ball so I started to run toward first base. I looked over to Patrick, Darby and Arvin to watch them cheer. Their jaws were dropped as low as their knees. I was so excited that I didn't realize that the bat never made contact with the ball. I struck out, we lost the game and I had to walk home by myself; no one would talk to me.

CHAPTER VI

LET"S TAKE A SHVITZ

My father, Barney and I had the same routine every Sunday; it started in January 1957. We had just moved into our new house in the suburbs. Barney and I shared a bedroom. We had bunk beds. He slept on the bottom; I slept on the top. Every Sunday morning at 9:00 A.M. my father woke us up and said "it's time for a good Shvitz". I was twelve years old the first time I heard that. I giggled. I thought he said "good shits". You take a *good shvitz* (perspire) at the Sauna. My father drove us in his Chevrolet station wagon to the Shvitz on William Street. The brown color station wagon had wood paneling on both sides. The back window could be raised up and the bottom lowered down; it was easy to get into the station wagon climbing through the back.

The Sauna was on the second floor of an old dilapidated house. We walked up a flight of stairs in a dark hallway. I passed through an old cracked wood door into a steaming hot room; the sauna. We sat in the sauna for approximately one-half hour. We were completely naked. Next we would walk a few feet, sit on an old wood bench and wait our turn.

We lay down on our stomachs on a narrow table. A hairy burly old man threw soapy water on us and brushed the water up and down our bodies. He used a large, soft feather brush. Then, we walked another few feet to a communal shower and rinsed. I was embarrassed. The old men, testicles drooping toward the ground, stood under the showers and gossiped about other people. I contributed nothing to the conversation. I shook my head in agreement with them. My schmeckle and testicles were smaller and balder than the old men. Barney's were just as small and bald.

I remember that the back door to the sauna was always left open. All of the houses behind the Shvitz were two stories high. The balconies were in the back of the houses on the same level as the Shvitz. The women and children stood on their balconies staring into the Shvitz. I could see and hear them laughing. The old men did not appear to be upset. I was upset! I hated the Shvitz! I dreaded Sunday mornings!

CHAPTER VII

MOYSHE"S BAR HAVZTIM
WINTER 1957

The Bar Havztim Speech

I n the past, a frequent gift at a Bar Havztim was a fountain pen. Before the popularity and price of today's ball-point pen, a fountain pen was a prized, cherished item not too far removed from a gold pocket watch. A Fountain Pen signified accomplishment, achievement and responsibility; a respectable position in life. The giving of the fountain pen was the acknowledgment of entry into adult life, with responsibilities that accompany it.

Bar Havztim marks a legal change of status, from childhood into adulthood, nothing more. This usually occurs when a Mensche Boy becomes 13 years old.

Saturday, March 2, 1957, I awoke at 8 AM in a cold sweat. I did not sleep a wink until ½ hour before I woke up. I tossed and turned because of the nightmare that I had. I dreamt of being born and then circumcised. It was a compilation of my personal experience

143

and all of the stories that I had heard about birth and *Brit Halim* of a *Mensche* boy.

I was either 13 years old or 9 years old on my Bar Havztim. Remember, I was born on February 29, which occurs every 4 years. I did not want to have an inferior age complex so I told everyone that I was thirteen years old. My older brother Barney, who would never by-pass a chance to tease me, told everyone that I was 9 years old; that I was just big for my age. My sister Marissa was thrilled and agreed because this would make her older than me.

It was a bitter sweet day. I was about to have my *Bar Havztim*, probably one of the most important days of my life. On the other hand, Bubby had died the previous week. We were both looking forward to sharing this day together. I knew that she would want me to continue on and she would watch over me from above. She always told me that life must go on. I certainly decided to obey her wishes.

On the day of a boy's Bar Havztim he declares."Today I am a Fountain Pen.

I did receive a Fountain Pen for my Bar Havztim. My Bar Havztim was on Saturday morning; there was a luncheon on that Saturday afternoon, held in the Temple (House of Worship) for the members of the congregation and my invited guests. Orthodox *Mensche* insists on eating only kosher food. The luncheon consisted of tuna fish, lox, bagels and assorted pastries, similar to food served at a *Brit Halim*. I was the "Guest of Honor". Most important to me, I was not going to be under the knife of the *Butcher*. I said a prayer after the luncheon. It was an extra prayer to assure that I wasn't going to be circumcised again. Ever since my *Brit Halim I feared being the "Guest of Honor" at any Event.*

During the Bar Havztim luncheon an uncle came up to me; he winked and he said to me, "NOW YOU WILL BECOME A FOUNTAIN PEN". I'm not sure what he meant; I thought that I BECAME FOUNTAIN PEN on the day of my Bar Havztim. I assumed it meant that I would someday have sex; not the same sex as *Bubby* had described it! This gave me more incentive to continue my quest to fulfill my true *Mission* in Life" to *shtoop*. It had the most influence on my life as I navigated through my early, middle and late teen years.

Let's digress for a moment and go back to the Bar Havztim ceremony. It was held at an Orthodox Temple. To this day I do not understand why my parents joined an Orthodox Temple. The only times I saw them in Temple were at Bar Havztim, *Mensche* weddings and *Mensche* funerals. They did not attend on *Rush Hanohsah* (New Year) or *Moy Ruppik* (Day of Atonement) Everyone in the *Mensche* Community attended services on those days, unless they were on their death beds or in the grave. Even on their death bed many Orthodox *Mensche* made an attempt to attend Temple services. My *Mensche* friends, Frankie and I made sure that we attended. It was an excuse not to go to school. The *Ibbar* (*Mensche* Religious Leader) led the congregation in prayer and the *Mensche* *Rotnac* (Religious Singer) chanted the hymns.

The morning of my Bar Havztim my family arrived by 8AM. The congregation arrived by 10AM even though services commenced by 9AM. The *Ibbar* called my parents and me to the *pulpit* (podium) at which time my parents presented a prayer shawl to me. I was proud as my father put the prayer shawl on my shoulders. It was custom that a boy could not wear *a prayer shawl* until his Bar Havztim. As the Bar Havztim Boy, it was my responsibility to read from the Tovrah (Books of *Mensche* History). For more than 3 years I studied the words to recite my portion of the Tovrah. My first task was to hold the prayer shawl fringes that dangled from both ends of the *shawl*. Then I touched and kissed the written portion of the Tovrah that I was expected to read that day. I began with the prayer before the reading of the Tovrah. I became nervous as I was preparing to read from the Tovrah. My brother Barney had his Bar Havztim before me so he gave me advice on how not to be nervous. He told me to take a deep breath, relax, look at the congregation with a sincere smile on my face and picture everyone in the congregation as wearing underwear. Picture the men in Tightie Whities and the women in red bras and crotch less panties. It worked! I was as cool as a cucumber as I breezed through my Tovrah readings. After the ceremony many of my aunts and uncles praised me on a flawless reading of the Tovrah and flawless chanting of the hymns. These were the aunts and uncles that slept through the ceremony. It was a good thing that they slept because they were a group of guests that couldn't make me nervous; they were asleep. I didn't have to picture them in their under wear as Barney had suggested. It would have been a really ugly picture!

That Saturday evening there was a party for my friends and young relatives. It took place in my honor at Pizza Tent Restaurant. The restaurant manager did not allow us to have a disc jockey to play music for our listening pleasure. They piped in music through their sound system which was tuned to Sandy Shores, a disc jockey on WKBV radio station. My guests had a choice to eat pizza with cheese or pizza with cheese and pepperoni. The *Ibbar* and *Rotnac* were not at the party so we were able to eat non kosher food.

The following Sunday afternoon a party was held in the Grand Ballroom of the Hotel Startlet in downtown Buffalo for my parent's friends; I was the "Guest of Honor".

My parents did not observe kosher. Shrimp cocktail was the appetizer followed by a salad and Yutz onion soup. The entrée was a choice of stuffed chicken, filet mignon or lobster tails. My *Bar Havztim* cake was served for dessert with coffee. The cake, shaped like a *Tovrah was* covered with vanilla frosting, decorated with bright blue icing.

After dinner a three piece band played the *Aroh,* a dance in which everyone stood in a circle, held hands and hopped back and forth, first to the left then to the right. My father, mother and I sat in separate chairs. A few strong guests lifted us into the air and laughed loudly when my mother fell off the chair when it reached the highest point.

On her way down she lost her rhinestone necklace and tore her low cut turquoise satin dress. She landed on the floor, broke the heel off her matching turquoise patent shoes and sprained her ankle. She did not laugh! The guests kept dancing. My father kept dancing until my mother yelled at him. "Michael move your tush over here and pick me up". The guests danced to slow and fast music.

The party ended at 11:12 PM; we went home. There were many gifts for me to open. The best gift was a 26", 10 speeds and bright red spin bicycle with streamers hanging from the rubber handles at both ends of the handle bar. There was a large rubber horn and a mirror mounted on the handle bar. I received many envelopes. There were no more gifts to open so I thanked everyone. My mother said that there was one more gift. She had been holding it for many weeks. It was a small rectangular box wrapped *in Bar Havztim* paper. I opened the envelope that was attached to the box. I read the note that was inside the envelope. I read it out loud.

My Dearest Moyshe,

This gift should have been given to you when you were born. It is a silver spoon for your mouth. You were always my favorite"

With all my Love,

Bubby

I looked around; there was not a dry eye in the room. My mother gave me a big hug and whispered into my ear. "You were always Bubby's favorite grandchild. She loved you more than any of her children. We both sobbed incessantly. I excused myself. I went to my bedroom and crawled into bed. I couldn't stop crying because I thought about Bubby who was no longer alive. I remembered that she had told me that "life goes on". So I closed my eyes and I played with myself before I fell asleep!

CHAPTER VIII

CRYSTAL BEACH COTTAGE

In 1948, my father wanted to buy a farm to live on during the summer months. He wanted to raise chickens for eggs, cows for milk; horses for manure and sheep. He never wore any wool clothing, so why would he want to raise sheep? I knew only one other reason to raise sheep. My parents had three children so I ruled out that reason!

My mother refused to live on a farm. Perhaps she didn't want to compete with sheep. She convinced him to buy a cottage in Crystal Beach, Ontario, Canada.

The 4" horizontal wood slats on the cottage were painted pink. The wood trim and shutters were painted orange. It had a small living room, one large bedroom and one small bedroom. My parents shared the small bedroom. Barney, Marissa and I shared the large bedroom. We flipped a coin to see who would get the bed. My father flipped the coin. Marissa called heads. She won. Barney and I had no idea that it was a two headed coin. My father winked at Marissa. .Barney and I slept on the floor. There was one small bathroom and a small kitchen.

There was not enough space in the kitchen for a refrigerator. The ice man delivered large blocks of ice that were placed in the left side of a two compartment basin. Food and milk was placed on top of the ice blocks. The Ice blocks were delivered twice a week.

Our clothes were placed in the right side compartment to be hand washed by my mother.

The clothes were hung to dry on a clothes line that extended from the back of the cottage to a branch of an old oak tree that had been planted in the grass thirty feet behind the cottage. Barney and I had the responsibility to watch for oncoming rain clouds so that my mother would be able to remove the clothes before the raindrops fell.

When Bubby was still alive she had the responsibility to count the wooden clothespins that secured the clothes to the line. We lost many clothes pins whenever a strong wind blew the clothes off the line. The clothes pins fell with the clothes.

CHAPTER IX

SWING IN SUMMER 1957

There is an amusement park and two public swimming beaches in the Village of Crystal Beach. Ashland Beach and Bay Beach are located on Lake Erie. At night we always went to Bay Beach. Families from Buffalo and Toronto, Ontario, Canada owned cottages in Crystal Beach. I went to Bay Beach to swim during the day and try to "get lucky" with the girls during the Evening.

There was a "hang out" in Crystal Beach for every one of all ages. The summer after my Bar Havztim was the first time that I went to the "hangout". It was known as the "Swing In" Dance Place. I thought it was the "Swingers In Dance Place" I was expecting to see men and women of all ages and all sizes dancing nude. I was disappointed! There were plenty of men, woman, guys and gals dancing. None of them were nude. There was an open air dance floor with the music, coming from a juke box, turned up very loud. The juke box was decorated with natural wood paneling and multi-color vertical tube lights blinking on and off as the 45 RPM records played. We all danced to the fast songs. We danced the 'jitterbug","twist" and "stroll".

Dorothy Jones, a "hot" sensual girl from Toronto went to the juke box; put twenty-five cents in the slot and selected three songs. Records played songs by many favorite artists. Johnny Mathis sang "A Certain Smile. Dorothy walked toward me and put her arms around my neck. I put my arms tightly around her upper back; pulling her body close to me. I could feel her kinipples harden against my chest. The song ended; Marty Robbins began to sing "Can't Help Falling in Love". Dorothy looked into my eyes with a certain smile, grabbed my tush and pulled me closer to her. I'm sure that she felt my *"schmeckle"* grow larger and harder. The song ended. Pat Boone began to sing "Love Letters in the Sand". Dorothy stopped dancing and whispered into my ear. "Let's go to Bay Beach and write letters in the sand or let's do something else". The three songs must have turned her on; they certainly turned her headlights on.

It was three short blocks away so we walked to the beach. I couldn't get there fast enough!

We arrived at the beach so we took off our shoes and walked on the cool sand to a secluded place on the beach. We didn't have a blanket; we didn't care! Dorothy and I lied down on the sand, my arm under her head; my body tight against her body. I leaned over and kissed her soft luscious lips. I put my hands on the bottom of her white cashmere sweater and I began to raise it over her head. She was not wearing a bra. She closed her eyes and I did the same after I stared at her firm perfectly round breasts for a few moments. Less than ten minutes later a bright light shined on our faces.

It was a police man holding a flashlight. He walked toward us; we jumped to our feet and ran back to the Swing In. Dorothy pulled the bottom of her sweater down to her waist as we ran. I did not become a Fountain Pen!

Jack's Stand, a snack bar which was only open during the summer months was at the entrance to Bay Beach. The owner was Jack Strak, a cab driver in Buffalo during the off season.

The only items on the menu were loose soupy scrambled eggs, very well done hamburgers, burnt hot dogs and greasy Yutz fries.

The food could not be cooked any other way. It was not gourmet food! We drank Loganberry drink, non-carbonated Orange drink or half and half (a combination of Loganberry and Orange).

A few friends and I met at Jack's Stand to meet a few girls. I hooked up with Elaine Bomgart. She wasn't the brightest girl that I ever met. Paul hooked up with Tania Slomwitz. We stopped for a drink at Jack's Stand before going onto Bay Beach. I paid for Elaine's drink because I thought that I was going to "get lucky". I changed from my clothes into my bathing suit in the Bath House on Bay Beach. The place was filthy. It didn't matter. I could look through a peep hole carved out of the thin wall that separated the men's room from the ladies' room. I got an eyeful watching the ladies change into their bathing suits. I saw all kinds of shapes and sizes, mostly extra large!

Paul, Tania Elaine and I went into the Beach House. We changed into our bathing suits. I peeped through the hole in the wall. We walked into the water until we were waist high. Elaine screamed "there's a shark in the water; she ran toward shore. That proved Elaine wasn't bright. Sharks don't swim in fresh water. They are salt water fish. Lake Erie is not salt water. I walked back toward the shore. Elaine kept running until she reached the car and jumped into the back seat of the car. I thought to myself" that could be a good sign. I opened the left side back door and I jumped into the back seat. She went out the door on the right side of the car. I sat in the back seat by myself. Paul and Tania were in the front seat. I suppose they were lying down because I couldn't see their heads. I don't know whose car it was. Paul, Tania, Elaine and I didn't have a car. We all jumped out of the car and we ran back to the Swing In.

My friends and I used to gamble; playing Black Jack ("21") on a picnic table next to Jack's Stand. We gambled on the table every day. I was lucky one day; I lost early. The Crystal Beach police "raided" the blackjack card game. Five of my friends ended up in jail. A Buffalo attorney put up the bail and helped them get out of jail. We didn't learn our lesson. The next day we continued to gamble on the table next to Jack's Stand. We bet on anything and everything. There was one outdoor bowling lane adjacent to Jack's Stand. There were no indoor lanes in Crystal Beach. Canadian bowling consisted of only five pins (known as "duck pins") and a small bowling ball with no holes. We bet on each ball thrown; $.50 for each pin that was knocked down, $1.00 for each spare; $2.00 for each strike and $5.00 for each high game.

The afternoon before my date with Terri Whinstone I gambled on the sandy beach with my friends. . We placed a blanket on the sand and played Black Jack. There was a term called "tapping the pot". Instead of betting a small amount, anyone could "tap the pot" to try to win all of the money that the dealer had in his "pot". If the person "tapped the pot" and won the hand he would become the dealer. The dealer played against everyone else. The odds were usually in favor of the dealer.

I remember specifically, a time when I said that I wanted to "tap the pot" and a voice behind me said, "NO YOU WON'T"! I was not aware that my father was standing behind me. Needless to say, he was not happy with my gambling. He embarrassed me as he shouted "leave the game".

I don't remember the punishment; other than the embarrassment that I suffered among my friends. It was another lesson, not well learned. After that incident, Terri cancelled the date.

I continued to gamble on the beach. Sammy's Snack Bar was located to the back of the beach; it gave Jack's Stand competition. I always thought that the Yutz fries were much better than any other; perhaps it was the mixture of salt, vinegar and sand from the beach.

CHAPTER X

SANDY WEINLOOSE

All winter and spring of 1958 I had worked out, lifting weights and exercising at Rite Form Gymnasium on Delaware Avenue in Buffalo. My "not so chiseled" body still looked good. I was thinner than I had ever been in my entire life. I was "very good looking," in my mind. My dark black, pompadour hair was shiny because I used more than one dab of cream. I was very confident with the skin that I was in. My four friends "were thankful. I was the "chick magnet" for all of us.

One of the girls that I befriended was seventeen years old. She wasn't beautiful not even a little bit beautiful. Sandy Weinloose was a *mieskeit* (ugly). That didn't matter because she had access to her father's 1956 Ford. She was one of the few people that knew I was not 16 years old. Although I didn't have a driver's license, she still taught me how to drive. Her father wrote the mileage of the car on a piece of paper when he left for work each day. After we drove to wherever we wanted, we drove the car to the gas station. We mounted the car onto a lift and put the car in reverse. Mileage would come off of the car when we drove in reverse. We kept track of the distance we drove and the distance from the gas station to her house, so we knew how many miles to "drive" the car in reverse, on the lift. Sandy was in "love" with me; maybe not in "love". At the very least, she had a "crush" on me.

Sandy couldn't attract any boys. I continued to be her friend because I wanted to drive her car. It took Sandy two months to realize that I was her "friend" because I only wanted to drive her car. She became despondent. The only way that Sandy could get a boy to like her she had to "put out". She became a *slooche.*

CHAPTER XI

TIFFANY

In the fall of 1958, Frankie drove us to Hamilton, Ontario, Canada, just across the border from Buffalo, New York. According to Frankie he was going to show us, as he called it, his "guilty pleasure". Frankie wanted us to visit a woman that he knew. We learned shortly after arriving in Hamilton that she was a prostitute. I would have bet a dollar to a dime that there were many prostitutes that lived closer to us; but we certainly didn't know any.

The five of us, that late evening, were sitting in Frankie's 1950 black Chevrolet. We were on a side street in Hamilton. It was dark and rain drops kept falling on the roof of the car. It was a heavy down pour. Perhaps Supreme Being was trying to tell us something.

Although it was a hot summer night, I couldn't stop shaking. Perhaps it was because of the heavy down pour of rain or I was nervous about meeting the prostitute and becoming a *Fountain Pen*. Frankie winked as he told us that she was going to charge us only five dollars each; this should have been our first hint as to how "classy" she was going to be. I was waiting for my turn. I was the youngest of the group. Frankie, Richard, Saul and Jacob went before I did. Jacob came back to the car, walking at a fast pace, continually looking backward over his shoulder. I have no idea why he kept looking backward over his shoulder. I asked myself; "Were the cops chasing him?" My heart beat faster when I heard a siren sound. It was not the cops.

I saw a fire engine speeding along the main street perpendicular to the street that we were on. Jacob entered the car and he told me the address on King Street. It was a four story apartment Building; I know that as fact. I walked up all four flights. There was no elevator. I walked through the very dimly lit hallway on the fourth floor, as quietly as possible. I heard very loud banging noises coming from behind each door of the apartments.

Finally, I arrived at apartment 6; it could have been an upside-down 9 because the number swung loosely on the door hanging by a small brad. I assumed it was a six because the hallway only had seven doors. I knocked quietly; not wanting to disturb the already noisy neighbors.

A woman appeared at the door dressed (or undressed) in a thin see-through black negligee. She introduced herself as Tiffany and smiled at me. I couldn't tell whether she was missing a few teeth or whether she was chewing blackjack gum. Tiffany my ass, I was sure that was not the given name that her parents blessed her with. She looked old enough to be my grandmother. She certainly did not speak a word of *Mensche. Tiffany's b*oobs were sagging toward the floor, lying on her balloon like belly. She invited me to enter the apartment.

The doorway opened up to a narrow hallway, barely wide enough for a thin person, facing side way to pass through. The hall way led directly in to the living room. Her voice was deeper than Tony the Tiger when he said. "GRRREAT"! She told me to sit on the red velvet chair and wait until she came back. Tiffany said that she had to do a very important thing. As she walked away from me, I thought that I was going to puke. I watched her naked dimpled ass jiggle up and down, like a bowl of jelly. I sat on the chair for a few minutes, which seemed to be like hours.

As I looked around the room I noticed two sconces hanging on the wall behind a red and black Mediterranean style couch. There were two black velvet throw pillows. The couch was centered between the two sconces that had red light bulbs in their sockets. There were no other lights in the room; therefore, the room was dimmer than the hallway. I heard a door open. I assumed it would be her coming back into the living room, Instead, I saw an old bald-headed man with no clothes on his body except for a torn undershirt, He was holding his *schmeckle* which appeared to be smaller than mine. His testicles were certainly larger than mine. I'm not positive because I certainly wasn't going to stare.

The old man rushed past me. I covered my mouth with my left hand. Fortunately, I did not puke.

Tiffany came back into the room wearing a red negligee; not the original black negligee. Perhaps it was a ritual to change negligees. I thought that I better hold on to my penis until I found out! After all, that old man held on to his.

Tiffany came in to the living room; walked over to me and took my hand as she led me across the room to what I thought would be the bedroom. Instead, she led me to the bathroom.

As Tiffany opened the door she handed me a bar of soap, wash cloth and two Trojan condoms. For the life of me, I couldn't understand why she gave me two condoms. I'm sure that she didn't realize it.

She demanded that I wash with the soap and hot water. I took off my pants and handed them to her. Fortunately, or not, I stood there in my boxer shorts; I was not commando that day.

Obediently, I entered the bathroom as she closed the door behind me. There was no lock on the door.

I scrubbed myself clean and of course, wiped myself dry. Not really knowing what to do next, I started to put on the condom. To my disappointment, I had trouble putting it on. In fact, the condom was probably too small; it broke as I tried to slip it over my testicles. What did I know? I took the second condom, peed in it and tied it up like a water balloon. I tossed it out of the bathroom window watching it fall four stories below. It exploded on the top of a convertible car. Luckily for the owner the top was up because of the rain.

I screamed to Tiffany through the bathroom door, saying that I could not come out. Eventually I did.

As I went past her she didn't even ask for the five dollars. Without hesitation I continued out of the apartment into the dim hallway, down the four flights of stairs and out of the door into the horrendous downpour of rain. I laughed to myself as I passed the broken condom on the top of the car roof.

Hastily, I walked toward our car looking backward over my shoulder, listening for the sound of police sirens.

A thought came into my mind. Is this what my uncle meant? If so, I was still not a Fountain Pen! I opened the car door and as I climbed in to the back seat Saul exclaimed. "That was great, wasn't it?" I didn't want to embarrass myself so I responded... "You went before me, what do you think?" We decided to drive to the Swiss Chalet in downtown Hamilton for a chicken sandwich, fries and drink.

We finished our meal. The bill came; I reached into my pocket for my twenty dollar bill. My pocket was empty.

That *shlooche (slut)* Tiffany; She stole my money. No wonder she didn't ask for the five dollars. She beat me for twenty. I had to borrow money to pay for my meal.

CHAPTER XII

ATLANTIC CITY

T he summer of 1958 was almost over. My friends, Adam Sternbaum, Stuart Pitterkin, Skip Tolou and I took a trip to Atlantic City, New Jersey. To my surprise, my parents let me go on the trip. I was only 15 years old. My friends were 17 years old. At that time there were no casinos in Atlantic City. We stayed in a two story hotel a few blocks away from the Boardwalk.

For fun, not realizing the danger, we jumped from the second floor balcony into the small swimming pool below. DO NOT TRY THIS.

The boardwalk had a phenomenal beach on the Atlantic Ocean. There were many restaurants, arcade games and girls.

The Boardwalk was crowded with College students. I had to live up to my reputation as a chick magnet" so I started a conversation with a group of college girls. It was no coincidence that most of them were pretty. Their tall legs reached as high as their necks, thin waists and watermelon size breasts earned them a 9 ½, if not a 10. Some of the girls agreed to meet us in the lobby of the Starlight Hotel at 9:00 PM. There were three of us and three of them. My mind was cluttered with thoughts of the orgy that I thought that we were going to have in their hotel room. Adam bought a bottle of liquor and I bought the grape juice to "brew" the "Purple Passion" drinks

One of the girls and Adam got drunk. There was no orgy. Stuart hooked up with Judy, a beautiful "bleached" blonde. She was approximately 5'7" tall.

Her measurements were approximately 36/22/38. I hooked up with Andrea, a brunette. She stood approximately 5'9" tall. Her measurements were approximately 32/34/34. Who was I to be choosy? Judy and Andrea wanted to go for a stroll on the boardwalk and the beach. We brought a blanket, which we took from Adam's bed. The four of us walked past an amusement ride named "Tunnel of Love". A boat floated through a very dark tunnel. The boat had three rows .Two people could sit across each row. Andrea and I sat in the second row; Stuart and Judy sat behind us. As we entered the very dark tunnel I heard a thump behind us. I looked back over my shoulder. Judy passed out; strewn across the back row. Her feet were on Stuart's lap.

I started to "make out" with Andrea. She put her arms around my neck and pulled my head toward her breasts. I was anticipating the taste of her succulent perky kinipples. It was so dark that I was not able to see a thing. Something seemed wrong. Andrea was moaning with pleasure before I began. Her kinipple was very large, almost what seemed to be the size of a thumb. Maybe she was holding her breasts. That couldn't be possible. Both of her arms and hands were on my neck. The boat floated past a dimly lit display of beautiful flowers. I could see a hand on Andrea's breast. With disgust I withdrew my mouth; it wasn't her kinipple, it was Stuart's thumb. He had reached over from his seat and fondled her right breast. She thought it was me that caressed her soft flabby breast. I felt like I gagged, it seemed like hours to reach the end of the ride. Finally, the ride was finished. Judy woke up and the four of us jumped out of the boat. Andrea wanted to leave; Judy didn't know what had happened! I convinced Andrea not to leave. The four of us continued on to stroll along the boardwalk. We came to a flight of stairs that lead down to the beach below the boardwalk. We spread the blanket on the sand. I lied down next to Andrea; Stuart lied next to Judy. I made sure that Stuart kept his distance. I don't know what Judy and Stuart were doing and I didn't care!

Andrea became very passionate as she kissed me and clawed at my back. I put my hand under her pink, cashmere sweater. I fumbled around trying to find the strap of her bra. I couldn't find it because she wasn't wearing a bra. Stuart must have left it on the boat. Fifteen minutes later I became confused. Andrea would not let me remove her shorts. I got up and walked toward the stairway to go to the top of the boardwalk. Stuart and Judy followed. Andrea remained on the blanket, not willing to join us.

The passion was very intense but it did not, as far as I was concerned, end to our mutual satisfaction. The girls went back to their hotel; Stuart and I went back to our hotel. We forgot to bring Adam's blanket. My testicles ached. This was the first time I experienced "blue balls"! Ask a male friend if you need an explanation. The vacation came to an end as did the summer; I still had not become a fountain pen!

CHAPTER XIII

HIGH SCHOOL

There was some good news; the Oskowitz Twins were going to be moving across the street from us on Allenhurst Road. They would be going to the same senior high school as me.

When school started in September (1959), we were freshman at Amherst Central Sr. High School. Marty's family did not move from Buffalo; he went to Bennett High School. I decided to join a *Mensche* fraternity, Pi Phi Alpha. It was similar to a social club. Every Wednesday we had a meeting to plan a Friday night party. Richard, Saul and Jacob joined the fraternity also. Frankie, the Nudnik, did not join. We tried to get him into the fraternity; the brothers checked us out. Frankie, of course, was not circumcised. So he was not allowed to join the fraternity. They did not want a token Nudnik. We liked Frankie; but we could care less that he was not allowed to join. We continued to be friends. Don't forget, we needed him to drive.

There was no hazing, unless it was considered hazing when we had to recite the Greek alphabet from beginning to end and from end to beginning, standing on our toes. The pledge master had a paddle so I was always afraid of being paddled. It never happened. At the first meeting I stood in a tight circle shoulder to shoulder with my pledge brothers. The pledge master was in the middle of the circle; holding a rope. A goose was tied to the rope that the pledge master held. The rope was tied around the goose's body and wings so that it could not fly. We were told to take off our pants. When we were all standing commando we feared that the goose was going to attack. The pledge master never let go of the rope. The rope was too short for the goose to reach us to chomp at our *schmeckles*. Saul, Richard, Jacob and I were going to quit the fraternity because of that stupid prank. The pledge master convinced us not to quit. He told us that it was the only prank that they ever did. He did not lie to us. We were glad that we did not quit.

Our fraternity had a basketball team. We were one of six teams in the basketball league. The games were played at the *Mensche* Center in downtown Buffalo. The championship game meant everything to us. We had never beaten the team that we played for the championship title. During that game the lead kept going back and forth. There was 20 seconds left to play in the game; we were ahead by one point. Ron, the best player on the other team was dribbling the ball down the court toward his basket. He had reached the foul line when I looked at the clock. It showed ten seconds left; the clock stopped. There was supposed to be two timekeepers. There was only one timekeeper at the table; it was one of our competitor's team members. Our timekeeper was busy flirting with a girl. Ron continued to dribble toward his basket; he scored with a layup shot. I looked up at the clock; I was confused the clock showed ten seconds left, it started to run again until the buzzer sounded the end of the game. We lost because the other team cheated. We protested to no avail; we could see ten dollars hanging out of the back pocket of the referee as he scurried off the court and out of the gymnasium door.

Although Frankie joined a different fraternity, we remained friends, until Saul and Richard got their drivers' licenses. Jacob and I continued to remain friends with Frankie. After all, we needed him as a backup if Saul or Richard couldn't drive us somewhere, anywhere.

Every Friday night there was a dance party; it was known as the "Eddie Fisher Coke Dance Party". Eddie was a well known singer who was married to Debbie Reynolds, a cute blonde singer-actress. They got divorced; Eddie married Elizabeth Taylor, a buxom brunette actress. She was probably thought of as being one of the most beautiful and sought after women on the planet, at least by every teenage boy that I knew. I had dreamed that I dated her and I became a FOUNTAIN PEN; then I woke up.

Let's get back to my story. The dance was sponsored by Coca Cola and they used Eddie Fisher's name because of his popularity with the teenage girls. I guess the executives at Coca Cola were smart enough to know that the boys would go to where the girls were. The admission cost $2 per person; the coca cola cost 50 cents per can. The potato chips and pretzels were free. We danced with the girls, holding them tight. We smooched until we got lucky enough to take the girls to the basement level. Actually, all we did was smooch there also. I was never lucky enough to become a FOUNTAIN PEN.

Throughout our freshman year I continued to date the twins; it was a wonderful friendship; never sexual. If I asked Judy for a date and she was not available, I would ask Jackie and if I asked Jackie for a date and she was not available, I would ask Judy. Neither one disapproved of the arrangement.

We studied together and encouraged each other to do well. The Twins were cheerleaders, on student council and active in other extracurricular school activities. They were very popular girls in school and they began dating different guys. We remained good friends; I began dating Anita Stein.

CHAPTER XIV

ANITA STEIN

Anita Stein and I were 15 years old. We were still riding bicycles and we didn't have our drivers' licenses yet. She was a few months older than me. Anita would probably have her license sooner than me. On a rainy Saturday afternoon, Arvin, Anita and I went to see a movie at Buffalo Theater on Main Street in downtown Buffalo. I had promised Arvin that Anita would "fix him up" with a date. He was disappointed when the date did not show up. We never told him that Anita never arranged for the date. However, we did accomplish what we wanted. Arvin drove us to the movie! Anita and I sat in the back seat of the car as Arvin drove. I noticed that he kept peering into his rear view mirror. Little did he know that he wouldn't see us shtooping. I treated Arvin and Anita to the movie. It cost $2.50 per ticket. It was cheaper than the cost of a taxi cab from our home to downtown Buffalo. We could have taken a bus for twenty-five cents each. Arvin bought his own popcorn. I treated Anita to a small box of popcorn and a drink. We sat in the last row of the balcony. Arvin was on my right, Anita on my left.

The movie was "House of Wax". I chose that movie because it was a horror movie showing in 3-D. I knew Anita would be afraid and she would need me to comfort her. I was not sure what comfort meant.

She had a cute figure. Her breasts were the size of my hands which I discovered at the movie when I *comforted* her. .After the movie we went to the Salad Bowl Restaurant in the Arrow Plaza on Delaware Avenue in Buffalo. There was a sign on the table; "twenty minutes maximum". It took the owner several months to realize that many teenagers would order a drink and nothing else while sitting at the table for hours at a time. It didn't take long for us to figure out why the waitress kept a stopwatch in her apron. I swear to Supreme Being, we were told to leave the restaurant exactly twenty minutes after sitting down, whether we finished our drink or not.

Anita Stein and I were in some of the same classes at Amherst Sr. High School.

In February 1960 we both took driver education classes together. If you passed the course there would be a 10% discount on automobile insurance and you could drive at night at 17 years old. You didn't have to wait until you were 18 years old.

We were in a driver education class on a December day. It was a dreary day with a light snowfall. There were four students and the instructor in the car. Two of us were sitting in the back seat of the driver education car. Anita was driving and the driver education instructor was in the front passenger seat to the right of her. Fortunately, he had a steering wheel and brake on his side of the car as a safety precaution in case a student driver lost control of the car. Anita Stein lost control. She skidded on an ice patch and the car hit a snow bank. The instructor was able to slow the car down so we did not slam into the snow bank too hard. No one was hurt and there was no damage to the car. Anita cried hysterically as the instructor told her that she failed the course!

In April 1960 I gave my fraternity pin to Anita. It was a significant gesture that I was seriously dating her exclusively. When a girl received a fraternity pin, she would wear it proudly on her blouse or sweater. The day after I gave it to her, I noticed that she was not wearing it. I thought that she had "broken up" with me. When I confronted her she explained that her father would be upset if he knew that she was dating only one boy. So, she wore the pin on her bra when she was home and she would wear it on her sweater when she was in school. Of course, I asked to see it. She said, "TRUST ME!"

I trusted her. The pin was on her bra.

We dated for several months. I spent a lot of time at her house, each day after school was finished. One afternoon, we were lying down next to each other on the brown leather couch in the family room. The radio was tuned to a station that featured romantic songs by Pat Boone, Johnny Mathis and other crooners. I began to take off her sweater and open the Buttons on her blouse. To my dismay, the fraternity pin was not on her bra. I really wasn't too discouraged; after all, I had her blouse off. She began to cry; I stopped immediately, I put on my shirt, I gave her a kiss on the cheek on her face, mot her ass and I walked out the door.

I told her that I would phone her that evening. I decided not to call her because I would see her in school the next day. I was pissed that I was not able to continue *comforting* her. I was just short of becoming a FOUNTAIN PEN! A few weeks later she told me that she had to stop dating me and she gave the pin back to me. I had no idea what the reason was. I asked her if it was because of what happened previously. She responded, "ABSOLUTELY NOT. Her father forbade her to continue to date me because her father had walked into her room when she was in the kitchen with her mother and he noticed the fraternity pin attached to her bra. He ran into the kitchen, bra in hand and asked what was going on?" At least he didn't wrap the bra around her head. She explained to her father that she was "in love" with me; NOT A GOOD ANSWER! After that I continued to see her in school; but, never again, elsewhere.

Actually, now that I think about it, I'm glad that he broke up our relationship. It gave me the opportunity to date other girls.

After every date when I came home, I wrapped my *schmeckle* in saran wrap; played with myself and went to sleep. I wrapped it in saran wrap because I didn't want to get the bed wet. Wax paper would have been too rough!

CHAPTER XV

CHARMAIGNE LAROSE

My brother Barney and I had been saving money for three years in order to take a ski trip to the Andes Mountains in Chile. That never happened; so in 1963 we went on a ski trip to St. Sauvieur Mountains in the Laurentians, north of Montreal. We vacationed for two weeks at the Nordique Lodge. It was an all inclusive vacation that included room, meals and ski lessons. Although it was February we were able to ski in shorts. The weather was an anomaly. The warm sun shone brightly. However the sun did not melt the snow; it only made the snow thicker.

At breakfast, the second morning of our vacation, Barney met Candice a 19 year good looking girl. I met Charmaigne Larose, an entertainer at the Yellow Canary Bistro Café in Montreal. Charmaigne was petite, about 5'1" tall, gorgeous blonde hair and a marvelous figure. Candice and Charmaigne were on vacation. They shared a room at the Nordique Lodge. Barney arranged to have dinner and dance with Candice for that evening. Charmaigne suggested that she and I drive to Montreal. She had to work that evening. She invited me to attend her performance insisted that I would enjoy watching and listening to her. Charmaigne called the owner of the Yellow Canary Bistro Café and arranged for me to have a table that was close to the stage. I thought, for sure that she had to be a stripper. We drove from the Lodge to Montreal in less than an hour. The speed limit on the Autobahn Highway was 80 mph. We arrived at the Café around 9:30PM. The entertainment did not start until 10:00 PM so we sat at the table and she ordered a split of Dom Perignon, very expensive champagne. She told me that she had to go backstage to change into her dress. The Master of Ceremonies introduced Charmaigne to the audience. She was not a stripper. The M.C. handed her the microphone. She stood center stage and looked over to me and winked as she began to sing her first song; "Feel Me Making Love".

Charmaigne looked stunning; her blonde hair was made up into a French Twist. Her deep red lipstick accentuated her light blue eyes. Her nicely apple sized breasts were exposed on the top in the low cut cherry red and silver-glitter dress. The tightly- fit dress showed off her extremely slender waist and shapely hips. Standing in high heels she appeared taller than 5'1"

She sang another half-dozen songs ending with the 1940's hit "I *Can't Stop Making Me Love"*. Charmaigne walked back to our table. She sat down beside me and whispered into my ear. "Let's finish our drinks and drive back to the Nordique Lodge. Candice had promised that she would not be in the room because she would be with Barney in his room. Charmaigne went backstage and changed into a comfortable outfit. She wore a white satin button down blouse. The top two buttons were open exposing cleavage and a portion of both round breasts. Her blue denim designer jeans fit snugly on her tiny tush and slender legs. I didn't like her choice of dark blue penny loafers and light blue wool socks, but I didn't say a word. We arrived at the Nordique Lodge by 2:00 A.M.

Charmaigne opened the door and escorted me into the bedroom. She suggested that I sit down and make myself comfortable while she changed into her see-through pink nightgown. She had no shame when she undressed in front of me and decided not to wear the night gown to bed. She slithered into bed and held the covers and blanket open for me to lie down next to her. I undressed and did as she asked! Facing each other, our warm bodies touched as she held me close. We kissed with slightly parted lips. I moved my right hand down her back, across her waist and up to her left breast. I caressed her firm round breast. She held my head and brought my lips to her hardened kinipple. Charmaigne cupped her breasts and held them together, as she asked me to kinibble on both kinipples. I did as she asked! She closed both of her eyes and purred with pleasure. My eyes slowly began to shut; probably due to the three glasses of Dom Perignon.

I opened my eyes when the light pierced through the window across from the bed. I noticed the clock on the night table next to the bed; it was 9:00 A.M. I couldn't believe it. I had fallen asleep. To my dismay, I did not become FOUNTAIN PEN that night. CLOSE; BUT NO KEWPIE DOLL!

Charmaigne scurried out of the bed, ran into the bathroom and began to shower. She did not ask me to join her in the shower. While she was dressing, I showered and dressed. We walked to the large dining room in the Lodge to have breakfast together. Barney and Candice were sharing a table enjoying their breakfast. There were two empty chairs so we joined them. The four of us decided to go skiing after we finished breakfast. We would meet at the top of Black Diamond ski slope. Charmaigne and Candice went to their room to change into their ski clothes. Barney and I went back to our room to do the same. We were putting on our ski boots when Barney, with a grin on his face, told me that Candice slept with him in our room last night and he got laid. I told him that Charmaigne and I slept in her room last night. I did not say another word.

We joined the girls on the slope, as planned. After four hours on the slope, the four of us decided to have lunch together. Charmaigne and Candice went into the dining room first; Barney and I followed about ten minutes later. We entered the dining room. Charmaigne and Candice were seated at a table for two people. Barney and I sat at the first empty table that we could find. It was a table for two, located across the room from the girls' table. The waiter brought me a note. I read it; "Thanks for the good time last night. With Love and Affection, Charmaigne"

I looked across the room; their table was empty. I assumed they went outside to ski. I never saw Charmaigne again!

Barney and I enjoyed the balance of our vacation, until we drove home. Barney was exhausted, probably from getting laid. He was sound asleep in the front passenger seat; I was driving.

We left Montreal at 11:00 P.M, on Friday night, heading west on Highway 401 driving toward Toronto. I had been at the wheel for approximately four hours maintaining the legal speed of 65 miles per hour. The road was covered with a light blanket of snow. There were some patches of ice underneath the snow. It was extremely dark because of the snow storm approaching or just because it was night time. The snow fell rapidly to the ground. Heavy wet snow accumulated on the front window of the car. The wiper blades were not moving rapidly enough to clear the snow off the windows. Barney was still asleep so I did not awake him. Although I was starting to tire,

My eyes closed for a few seconds. I heard a loud screech; Barney awoke; screaming loudly and shaking me while holding my right shoulder. The car had done an180 degrees turn. We were on the other side of the highway. Our car was facing east. I did not realize that I had fallen asleep. Fortunately no one was injured and there was no damage to the car. Unfortunately, neither one of us wanted to drive. We fought over how we would get home. Barney wanted to burn the car and leave it on the side of the highway. We did not have insurance. I wanted to have the car towed. I won. It cost us $1,800 to tow the car home. We sold it for $1,600.

CHAPTER XVI

ISSING BRIDGE SKI RESORT

The following March, there was still snow on the small mountains of Kissing Bridge Ski Resort in Colden, New York; thirty miles west of Buffalo. Barney and I went skiing on a Saturday morning. There were two long lines of skiers waiting to take the four-seat chairs that took skiers to the top of the mountain. We approached the first chair on the lift that was available. Barney and I jumped onto the left side of the chairlift. Two girls jumped on to the right side. They were both dressed in white ski outfits, white ski caps, white scarves, white gloves and dark tinted goggles. It was impossible to see whether or not they were good looking. Their faces were hidden by the ski caps, scarves and goggles. Barney and I assumed that they were as inquisitive about our looks as we were of their looks.

The four of us ascended the mountain and jumped off the chairlift at the top. We were very friendly with each other, so we decided to ski on the slopes together. We were anxious to do as much skiing as possible; we forgot to introduce ourselves to each other. The slopes were very crowded so we only took one run down the slope. At the bottom of the slope we agreed to go into the dining room for lunch. The girls were able to get out of their skis sooner than Barney and me, so they proceeded to the dining room first. We entered the dining room and we spotted the two matching white ski outfits. The girls were not wearing their ski caps, scarves and goggles. Barney and I recognized them. We put our ski caps, scarves, goggles and gloves into an empty locker. There were two empty seats at their table so we joined them.

What were the odds? Seated across from each other; our caps, scarves and goggles were not covering our faces. Barney exclaimed that the taller girl was Candice, the girl he shtooped in the Laurentians. She was very amiable. Candice introduced her friend Joanne to Barney and to me. We chatted for approximately one hour. Joanne lived in West Seneca, New York, not far from Buffalo. Candice was visiting her so they decided to go skiing at Kissing Bridge. We decided to ski on the slopes together. Two of us waited in the left line and two of us waited in the right line of the four-seat chairlift. Barney and Candice sat on the left side. Joanne and I sat on the right side.

Barney and Candice agreed to hook up later that evening. I had already made arrangements for the evening. Joanne had to fend for herself. I had driven my own car and Barney had driven his own car to Kissing Bridge so transportation was not a problem. I left the resort at 5:00 P.M. I don't know what time Barney left. I arrived home at approximately 6:00P.M. I showered, shaved and dressed for my date with Vera. We were going to dine and dance at the upscale Primo Restorante in Williamsville, New York, a suburb of Buffalo. Vera and I danced until 1:00 AM. I had wondered whether that was the night that I would become a Fountain Pen. She showed me a text message that she received ten minutes earlier. Her mother had become ill. I speeded all the way to her house. I dropped her off and I went home alone. I arrived home at approximately 1:45 A.M. Barney's car was in the driveway.

I approached the front door and I opened it as quietly as possible. I assumed that Barney had to be sound asleep. I entered my house. I heard voices coming from my parent's bedroom. It couldn't be my parents. They were in Mexico on vacation. I walked quietly toward my parent's bedroom in case there were intruders in the house. I didn't want them to hear me. I began to call 911. I reached for the bedroom door. I opened it very quietly. I saw some silhouettes lying on the bed. Barney was lying on his back; Candice was kissing him on the mouth, her legs dangling off the side of the bed; Joanne was humming. I saw the back of her head. Her hands were on Candice's ass. Her feet were dangling off the bottom edge of the bed. Barney was having a threesome. I was pissed. I still had not even become a Fountain Pen. I quietly closed the bedroom door and I tip-toed to my own bedroom so that they wouldn't know that I was home.

I undressed and crawled into my comfortable bed. I was alone. I was not sure whether I should fall asleep or play with myself. I decided to wrap my schmeckle in saran wrap. I fell asleep 10 minutes later. I awoke at 11:00 A.M. I did not awake Barney until 11:30 A.M. We went for breakfast at the International House of Kishka. I had put whipped cream on my pancakes when Barney remarked, "Moyshe that whipped cream reminds me. I had a threesome last night". That *Puhtz,* I couldn't eat my kishka. He queried as to why I was not eating my kishka. I told him that I knew he had a threesome. Barney had a perplexed look on his face. I wouldn't give him the satisfaction to let him know that I saw him in my parent's bedroom with the two girls. I didn't say another word!

CHAPTER XVII

MENSCHE BS STATE COLLEGE

T he *Mensche* community grew rapidly in Buffalo during the 1950's so *Mensche* BS State (BS), a two year college was founded to accommodate the growing population. I applied to BS. I was accepted.

Grandfather Herman was the first professor to teach a course in history *about hanging wallpaper*. BS had a policy of admitting former professors' descendants no matter what their grades were in High School

Wallpaper 101 History of Wallpaper was a required course in the first semester. *Wallpaper 102 Hanging Wallpaper* was a required course in the second semester. Two languages, *Mensche* 101 and English 101 were required courses in the first semester. All four courses were very boring. I had already learned everything about hanging wallpaper from my father. I had already learned *Mensche*, except the swear words, from Bubby. English 101 was all about English prepositions. English 102 was all about English nouns.

I met Rita Harpowitz the second semester. Rita was a buxom red head. She was a bright student. Her major was English. Among other things, I learned everything about prepositions and nouns from Rita. She invited me to her dormitory room once a week for six weeks to teach me about the female anatomy. She told me that she would explain to me what excited her when she was on a date or lying on her bed at home, alone with the lights turned off. She enjoyed doing things in the dark.

On Monday, week one she took off her shoes, her feet were bare and she told me to put each of her toes in my mouth. She wanted me to lick and kinibble on them. I don't know why I waited to ask her beforehand whether she washed her feet and toes. On Monday on week two she rolled up her slacks to her knees and told me to gently pat each knee; I had no idea why she enjoyed that.

On Monday, week three she took off her slacks; she told me to watch her exercise on the thigh master. On Monday, week four she took off her blouse and bra. She told me to stare at her. On Monday, week five she took off all of her clothes, told me to lie down next to her on the couch and close my eyes. She put my hands on her breasts and told me to caress both of her breasts. Then she told me to open my eyes because she had something important to ask me. I was excited. She probably wanted to ask me to shtoop her. She asked "will you come back on Monday, week six? I will teach you more prepositions and nouns?"

What a bummer, I still had not become a Fountain Pen!

I had enough BS so I quit school and the following year I applied to the State University of New York at Buffalo (UB), a four year college. Although I earned twelve credits for passing the courses with a 3.65 average at BS, the credits were not transferred to UB.

STATE UNIVERSITY OF NEW YORK AT BUFFALO (UB)

I was in line waiting to register for classes. I heard three familiar voices yell "Moyshe Tushman". To my surprise it was Frankie, Jacob and Saul. Jacob's family had moved to Rochester; Saul's family had moved to Syracuse; I thought that Frankie had joined the army. I was wrong! They heard that I was accepted (UB. They wanted to renew our friendship so they applied to UB.

We looked around the room; perhaps Richard had applied to UB. He was standing at the other end of the room. In unison we yelled "Dick". Everyone in the room stared at us. We were together, FOUR MENSCHE – ONE NUDNIK.

Frankie still had sleek, greasy, ebony black color hair combed backward to form a D.A. in the back of his head. His well-sculpted body was proof that he continued to lift weights and he probably maintained that strict diet of chicken and vegetables. Frankie was not the tallest of our group. He didn't grow shorter. Richard grew taller.

Richard did not have a Buzz cut He was partially bald. He was still thinner than Frankie.

Saul was still shorter than Richard. Saul's sandy brown color hair was not combed and probably never washed. He was still fat and he had a distinct odor on his body, not as bad as when we were younger. He had been the shortest of our group when we were younger .He grew several inches; now he was as tall as Richard.

Jacob was shorter than Saul. His well groomed dark blonde color hair was not longer than Frankie's hair. Jacob was much thinner than Saul. He had put on several pounds.

I was approximately the same height and weight as Richard when we were younger. In college I was about the same height as Richard but I had become a bit heavier. My dark black color hair was short and well groomed with a part on the left side. Hygiene was very important to me when we were younger and it was still important to me in college. I didn't use Old Spice in college as I did when we were younger. I changed to *Obsession for Men* after I showered and shaved. I brushed my teeth immediately upon waking up in the morning. I brushed my teeth after every meal and before I went to sleep. *B*ubby insisted when I was younger so I continued to do the same in college.

The first four semesters at UB I made the Dean's List. My grade point average was 3.5 in Calculus, Ancient History, Political Science and Physics. I failed gym class. . I had a heavy schedule in my freshman and sophomore years. I decided to take a few easy courses in my junior year. Geography, anthropology, physical education and sex education were the easiest courses available. I signed up! Those classes were the largest mistakes of my college years!

The first day of Physical Education I walked into the men's locker room, undressed and put on my blue UB T-shirt, blue UB shorts and blue sneakers. I looked like a member of the Blue Men Group. Completely dressed, I walked from the men's locker room toward a sign marked Gymnasium. I did not have my eye glasses on. I did not notice that the Gymnasium sign was to the right of the ladies' locker room. I walked into the ladies' locker room by mistake. Several of the girls were only covered with their bra and panties. Many other girls were completely nude. Several of the girls ran and hid behind the lockers. Several ran toward me. I believed that this was going to be my lucky day. I was going to become a FOUNTAIN PEN! I was surrounded by four completely nude girls. Three girls held my hands tightly against the cold steel gray lockers. Was the third girl going to do more? She did! She lowered her head, grabbed my ankles and held them tightly against the gray cold steel lockers.

I heard the shrill loud sound a whistle. Five husky campus policemen rushed into the locker room. They dragged me across campus to an enclosed area. The area was enclosed by black iron vertical cabinets. A campus policeman asked me several questions. I answered his incriminating rude questions. A Buffalo policeman entered the room. I explained "I meant no harm. I had lost my glasses in the men's locker room and I inadvertently walked into the ladies' locker room because I was as blind as a bat without my glasses." I showed him my student identification card. He verified that I was a student. Fortunately, another policeman walked into the room holding my glasses. They believed my story. They let me go and told me to be more careful, not to lose my glasses. I was upset; not because of the questioning; it was because I crapped in my pants. I missed class! Worse, I did not become a Fountain Pen.

The following week I was more careful, I did not misplace my glasses. The Phys Ed instructor confronted me before I entered the gym. I explained the reason that I was absent from class the previous week. He accepted my explanation, but he did tell me that I would be expelled from his course if I was absent two more times.

I entered the gym. I was really pissed. There were two heavy braided ropes hanging from the ceiling. The ceiling was higher than the ceiling in School #81. There was no way that I would be "King Kong". I was not able to join the monkey club. I never reached the top. I never grabbed the flag. I skipped the next class. I knew that if I missed one more class the instructor would expel me from his course. The following week I walked past the gymnasium on my way to anthropology class. I looked into the gym; the ropes were not hanging from the ceiling. I did not gym class!

Anthropology was not as easy a subject as I had thought. I read the description of the course when I registered. I had the understanding that Anthropology was the study of the science that deals with the origins, social customs and beliefs of human mankind. The description was misleading!

The course was actually the study of human beings' similarity to other animals I attended three classes. I couldn't understand a thing. I quit the class.

Geography was the study of the land including climate, elevation, vegetation, population and topographical features of the Earth and Planets. I couldn't understand a thing. I quit the class.

Richard, Saul, Jacob, Frankie and I took the geography course. We were able to register for the class that was on the same day and same time. It worked out perfectly. The class was on Mondays at 9:00 AM. Richard and I didn't have to skip any geography classes to make our daily 11:00 AM breakfast at the International House of Kishka.

Professor Everlast taught geography course. It was very interesting the entire week that he taught geography about the planets and the effect they had on earth's surface. He wore different costumes. The planets' names were derived from Greek/Roman mythology. Earth is the only planet that does not derive its name from mythology.

Mercury is the Supreme Being of commerce, travel and thievery in Roman mythology so Professor Everlast dressed as a traveling snake oil salesman.

Venus is the Roman Goddess of love and beauty so Professor Everlast dressed in a dark lavender robe and wore a tiara on the female wig that was on his head.

Earth derives its name from Old English. Professor Everlast wore a Globe of the earth on his head. Jupiter was the King of the

Supreme Beings in Roman mythology. Professor Everlast wore a picture of a burning bush attached to the front of his T-shirt.

Mars (Ares) is the Roman Supreme Being of War. Professor Everlast held a deep red (color of Mars) spear as he lectured about the effect of Mars' gasses on Earth.

Saturn is the Roman Supreme Being of agriculture. Professor Everlast wore a string of corn around his neck.

Uranus is the ancient Roman deity of the Heavens, the earliest Supreme Being. Professor Everlast rode into class on an *ass* (donkey).

Neptune (Poseidon) was the Roman Supreme Being of the Sea. Professor Everlast wore a fish around his neck and he held a three pronged spear

Pluto (Hades) is the Roman Supreme Being of the underworld in Roman mythology. Professor Everlast wore a devil's costume.

Everyone was able to associate these costumes with the planets and their effect on earth.

I enjoyed geography more than any course that I had ever taken. Mr. Everlast drew many pictures and graphs on the chalk board. The pictures of earth showed land elevations and climate changes, elevation, vegetation, population and topographical features of the Earth and Planets.

I was perplexed as to the vast amount of information that he offered and I wasn't sure what questions he would ask on the quizzes because of the amount of information.

I did not want to miss a single detail so I took an abundance of notes. I took notes in class and I wrote notes from the text book. I drew charts, pictures and graphs in color pencils. My notes were phenomenal. My notes became a notebook. The notes were 263 pages long. Other students wanted to borrow the notebook. They wanted to pay rent to me for use of the notes. I loaned the notes to Richard, Saul, Jacob and Frankie. They got an "A" in the course. I got a "C". I was so busy doing the notes that I didn't have time to study.

Richard and I had breakfast at the International House of Kishka every morning. One morning when we became very involved in conversation I did not notice the time. I missed my gym class. That was three times. The physical education instructor expelled me from his class. I pleaded with him. He told me that he would give me an opportunity to pass his class. I had to show up the following week and run around the school track two times. The track was approximately one-quarter mile.

I needed my energy. Richard and I had breakfast the morning that I was supposed to run around the track. Joanna Sternstein came into the restaurant and asked us to join her and Susan Rosenstern to study in their dormitory room. It was still early. I had plenty of time before I had to run track. Joanna, Richard and I drove to the dormitory to meet with Susan.

We entered the room. Susan was sitting on a black leather couch. She patted the couch and told Richard to sit down next to her. Joanna sat on the couch next to Susan. There was room on the couch for me to sit next to Joanna. Richard and Susan began to kiss; Joanna and I began to kiss. It was strange. Precisely at the same time Susan pulled away from Richard and Joanna pulled away from me. The girls faced each other, smiled and began to kiss. Joanna unbuttoned Susan's light orange color blouse. She began to caress Susan's left breast. Then she wet her pointer finger and circled Susan's hard dark pink kinipple on her right breast. I sat on the couch and I reached for Joanne's left breast. She shoved my hand away from her and she continued with Susan. My *schmeckle* grew larger and harder; it was a waste of a good boner. Richard and I jumped off the couch and walked toward the door. Susan asked us to stay and watch. We did! I lost track of the time, it was too late to go to run around the track. Three times, I struck out. The instructor gave me an "F" in the course.

The following Friday Jacob introduced me to Jamie Sunstone, a transfer student from Oneida College. Jacob told me that he had heard that she was the dumbest and horniest girl at college. I asked her for a date. I invited her to go to watch the "submarine" races at Point Albino. Jamie accepted the date. She was certainly dumb! Point Albino is the western most point in Crystal Beach, situated on Lake Erie. I told Jamie that the car was facing the water so that we could watch the "submarine" races that were going to start in a few hours. We could keep our selves busy listening to music on the car radio and dance on the grass next to the car.

I did that to get her out of the front seat. We danced for a few minutes. I suggested that we get into the back seat of the car. It was starting to get dark. Although the top two buttons of Jamie's blouse were already unbuttoned, I couldn't see her breasts. I saw her very unidentifiable cleavage which appeared to have a small amount of hair; in the dark I couldn't tell for sure.

We were in the back seat and we started to kiss passionately. I thought to myself what Jacob had said. I already knew that Jamie was dumb and horny because Jacob had told me. I decided to forget any foreplay. I put my hand on her thigh which felt a little chafed; probably from shaving for her bathing suit "summer cut". I reached into her panties.

She had a *"schmeckle"*; I withdrew my hand immediately. This was my biggest fear; SHE WAS A HE! JAMIE WAS A JAMES!

As I jumped out of the car, I grabbed the long dark brown color wig off his head. I ran toward Lake Erie and I threw the wig in the water. I could see it start to sink toward the bottom of the lake so I walked back to the car.

The ride back to Buffalo took less than thirty-five minutes. The ride usually took sixty minutes.

CHAPTER XIX

PI EPSILON ALPHA FRATERNITY)

Saul, Richard, Jacob and I joined Pi Epsilon Alpha Fraternity. It was a *Mensche* Fraternity; Frankie could not join so he joined Mu Alpha Sigma Fraternity. It was a Nudnik Fraternity. At least we were all at UB together. Saul and Jacob were very studious. They spent a lot of time together in the library. Richard and I were not as studious; we did a lot of non-academic things together. Frankie joined Saul and Jacob more often than Richard and me.

Richard and I were very active in fraternity activities. Quite often we ate breakfast at International House of Kishka. Actually we skipped our 11:00 A.M. class so that we wouldn't miss eating breakfast every Monday, Wednesday and Friday. We became very friendly with Chuck, the restaurant manager; he allowed us the opportunity to hold a kishka eating contest for our fraternity brothers. Richard and I determined odds for each contestant so that the Fraternity Brothers could bet on who would win. The betting pool amounted to $6,500. Chuck did not tell us that National Headquarters had not approved the contest. It was cancelled. The Brothers never questioned what happened to the money.

We frequented Batavia Downs Horse Racing Track; every Monday through Friday night. The problem was that the first time we went to the track, we won $1,400. That winning hooked us. Richard and I thought that it was easy money. We couldn't and wouldn't lose. *OY VEY* we were wrong! The first bet was to win, every bet after that was to break out even! Richard lived in the dorms and I lived at home. I told my parents that Richard and I were going to the library to study each night; we actually went to the track.

One evening Robert, a Fraternity Pledge asked to join us. He was only seventeen years old. You could not get into the track unless you were at least eighteen years old. The three of us were at the entrance gate. Robert was not allowed to enter the track. We escorted Robert to my car and we insisted that he wait in the car until we came back after the races were finished. Approximately two hours later the races finished; Richard and I walked to the car; Robert was waiting in the car for us to come back. He told us that he had plenty of time to think while he was sitting in the car. He had figured a way to get into the track. We promised to take him to the track the next day.

We arrived at the track; Robert was sitting in the back seat putting something on his face just above his upper lip and just below his nose. He was putting on a fake mustache. He appeared to be twenty-two years old. The three of us went into the track. He was a neophyte so we let him chose the horses to win the race. We won five of eight races. We had enough money to last us the next two weeks. That was enough for a lot of kishka. On the way out of the track his mustache fell off. A security guard stopped him and brought him inside to the security office. The officer took his picture to place on a board located at the front gate. As punishment, Robert was banned from the track for one month. The security guard at the front gate could compare the picture to everyone coming to the entrance to determine who was banned from the track.

The following year, UB lowered the cost of tuition to $250 per semester. It was affordable for many more students. The campus swarmed with many guys and gals from New York City. Many were *Mensche* chicks; the pickings were aplenty.

Pi Epsilon Alpha Fraternity had many parties. There was a social party for co-eds. The girls from NYC were game to attend many of our events, especially the toga parties. We danced the twist, the mashed potatoes, the locomotion, the stroll and the hop, among other dances. We dressed in white bed sheets (togas) with no clothes underneath. Our toga parties were held every Saturday night.

The parties were held in a large room on the second floor of Washington Hall. A silver glass mirror ball hung from the middle of the ceiling. White strobe lights shined on the ball as it turned. Small spots of light appeared throughout the room, landing on the ceilings, on the walls and on the entertainers and dancers. Many times there were "has-been" singers entertaining the attendants. Richard and I were in charge of arranging transportation and accommodations for the entertainer. I owned a 1962 Chevrolet Corvair. I owned one of the few cars in our fraternity. We escorted our guest, squeezing the entertainer into the back seat of my small two door silver blue car. I threw his suitcase into the trunk of the car. The trunk was in the front of the car. The engine was in the back. Richard and I usually brought a bottle of Thunderbird wine and pretzels for our guest. Accommodations were usually at a small, sleazy motel in downtown Buffalo. The room cost $15 per night or $4 per hour.

Let's digress to the party. There was a small room adjacent to the large room. It had a wooden door that could only be locked from the inside with a brass bolt attached to a chain. The more adventurous entered the room to enjoy a private party. Richard and I were always anxious to partake. The best party that we ever had was held on the last Friday night, closest to the end of the second semester in our third year at UB. In the small room there was a wet toga party for guys and gals. We told the girls that we had a ritual. It was *Musical Chairs with a hitch.*

There were fourteen of us in the small room. We threw buckets of warm water on each other. Richard and twelve other students were sitting on 14 chairs. They were sitting guy, gal alternating next to each other. What the hell! I decided to join. The only space available was between two chunky girls. I sauntered over and sat down between them. Matilda was *zaftikeh moid* (chunky but pretty). She was on my left side, Wilhelmina the *mieskeit* (ugly) girl was on my right side. Each person held the left hand of the person to their right. The music started off fast. The "Game" was a new version of "Musical Chairs". We acted like elementary school children. The "Bunny Hop" was the first dance. Every one stood up and did the Bunny Hop" around the chairs. When the music stopped we paired off with the person that was to our left and we grabbed a chair to sit on together. The next song was "The Twist" Everyone "twisted" around the chairs. The music stopped and each couple tried to grab a chair to sit on together. There were only five chairs. That continued through four more dances: "Mashed Potatoes", "Jitterbug", "Chicken Dance" and "The Stroll. Of course, I was forced to pair up with Matilda. We were the last couple standing; we lost. We had to disrobe our togas and wrestle in a pool of jello in front of everyone in the room.

I closed my eyes and pretended that I was with Elizabeth Taylor. We were lying side by side facing each other. I moved my fingers from her flabby thighs up to the handle bars on the sides of her soft flabby stomach. There was no way that I was with Elizabeth Taylor.

Matilda's warm breasts pressed against my chest. I rolled her onto her back and I pinned her. I literally jumped on top of her. I slid down until my mouth reached her breasts. I drooled as I licked the cleavage between her breasts. I could feel her hands as she grabbed the outer sides of her breasts. Matilda pushed her breasts toward my cheeks. My tongue was trapped in the cleavage of her breasts. She squeezed harder and pushed her breasts against my cheeks. I could hardly breathe.

I licked the orange jello off her body. It didn't taste too bad. However my favorite flavor was cherry.

The area around my groin became warm. My *schmeckle* became the size of a short stub of celery as she pushed her breasts together. I did not see Richard standing over us. He poured a bucket of ice cold water on us. My *schmeckle* shrunk to the size of a baby carrot. Every one applauded. I opened my eyes. This was not a dream, it was a nightmare!

Bubby was wrong. She had told me that no one lost when a boy and a girl were naked and they wrestled. I was on top but I lost. I still didn't become a Fountain Pen!

Mathilda and I ran out into the dark stormy rain. We got caught in the down pour. It washed the sticky orange jello off our bodies.

During the spring, Pi Epsilon Alpha Fraternity had a special weekend planned for the brothers and their dates. It was held at the Nevelle Country Club.

The Nevelle Country Club was in the Catskill Mountains. I drove my 1962 Corvair with five other passengers. The car could only accommodate a total of five small people. It was crowded to say the least. Richard was in the front passenger seat. The car had bucket seats in the front. My date Rochelle sat between Richard and me. She sat atop the crack between the bucket seats. The stick shift was on the floor, between her legs. Every time I maneuvered the shift, she had to maneuver her legs. There were three passengers in the rear seat. Fortunately for them it was a bench seat. They still had to sit close together, shoulder to shoulder with no room to move. It was supposed to be a six hour drive from Buffalo to the Nevelle. The New York State Thruway was a flat highway until it reached the mountains.

We approached the first stretch of road that was not flat. It was difficult to ascend the steep slope. The car was in third gear when it slowed down and began to roll backward. The car was weighted down with too many people. Two people decided to get out of the car and walk two miles until the road flattened. The car was able to move forward with only three people in the car. The drive to the Nevelle usually took six hours. That drive took eight hours.

We arrived at the Nevelle at 9:00 PM. The clerk at the front desk told us that check-in was supposed to be 6:00 PM. It was too late for dinner so we didn't eat that evening. That was a good thing; our stomachs did not protrude when we undressed in front of our dates. We shared rooms with our dates. Although everyone else had sex, Rochelle and I didn't. We were in bed next to each other when I remembered that her father had warned me before we left Buffalo. "If you get fresh with my daughter, her older brother Jonathan will have your hide." He was four inches taller and forty pounds heavier than me. I fell asleep immediately. I thought that I would become a Fountain Pen that night. I was wrong! The next day we had an ice skating party. A few of the Brothers' dates did not know how to ice skate, so they went back to their rooms with their dates, Those Brothers got lucky!

Dinner was held at 7:00 PM. The plates were filled with prime ribs, twice baked potatoes, kishka and an assortment of vegetables. Delicious strawberry shortcake was dessert. After dinner, we danced to the music of a three piece band. The dance was over by 11:00 PM. We went to our rooms to retire for the night. Rochelle promised that she would not say a word to her father. We kissed with parted lips, her tongue was down my throat; my tongue penetrated her throat. I began to caress her breasts. My hands slid down her sides. I was ready to pull her pajama bottoms down below her waist.

She reached for my hands and stopped me with tears in her eyes. It was her time of the month. I said "SO WHAT!" She slapped me and she turned on her side with her back pressed against my back. I fell asleep. The next morning we awoke at 9:00 AM. I leaned over and I tried to kiss her on the cheek. Rochelle turned her face away from me. She showered by herself and dressed in the bathroom.

I asked if she was upset with me. She said "I wasn't until you said SO WHAT!" Once again, it could have been a perfect opportunity.

However, I was still not a Fountain Pen! We went to breakfast. Everyone was smiling and laughing except me.

We drove back to Buffalo; it seemed like twelve hours. Rochelle and I did not say a word to each other. I brought her home. Rochelle's father was waiting in the driveway. I dropped Rochelle off and as I drove away. I told her father to relax. Jonathan did not have to bruise his hands on my face. That was my last date with Rochelle.

The following year Saul had a bright idea. The fraternity brothers would challenge the U.S. Post Office in a race to deliver mail. The Post office had nothing to gain to accept the challenge. The Post Office had no idea that there was going to be a race. Saul contacted a reporter at the Buffalo Courier Express. He told the reporter that the brothers of Pi Epsilon Alpha were going to mail a letter from the Buffalo Post Office to Geneva, NY at 8:00 AM on Monday, September 15. The Brothers would take a letter from Buffalo to Geneva by bicycle on September 15 at 8:00 AM. The reporter had one camera man at the starting point and one camera man at the end point to record the challenge. The day before the competition the Brothers lined up bicycles along the NYS Thruway. Each bicycle was five miles apart for the Brothers to ride. They had a relay race to see if they could beat the mail carriers. The U.S. Post Office delivered the letter at 10:00 AM on September 16. Pi Epsilon Alpha Fraternity brothers delivered their letter within 10 hours on September 15, the same day the competition started. There was an article and picture of the Pi Epsilon Alpha brothers standing at the Geneva Post Office. The article and picture was in the Courier Express newspaper declaring "COLLEGE FRATERNITY BICYCLERS BEAT U.S.POST OFFICE AIRPLANES IN MAIL DELIVERY COMPETITION". There was no mention that a letter carried by airplane could not reach its destination until the next day because the airplane only flies over night! I did not partake in the race because I knew that there would not be any girls in the competition. There were forty brothers in the race. Therefore their girl friends were alone in Buffalo for me to hit on. It didn't matter, I came down with the flu; I was bed-ridden the entire time.

Richard and I played many pranks on the pledges. We did not prank Robert because he was such a good sport at Batavia Downs.

Pledge Stuart was a wise guy. He continually bragged that he could outsmart any Fraternity Brother Richard and I had Stuart in the back seat of my car. We blindfolded him. Then we drove to the foot of the Peace Bridge in Buffalo. The Peace Bridge connected Buffalo and Fort Erie Canada. The Customs authorities were very liberal and it was not a disadvantage that Richard and Customs Agent Trent's son were good friends from Commonwealth Avenue. We told him about our prank. He advised us to pass through his line to enter Canada. Richard and I decided to teach Stuart a lesson. We removed the blindfold and instructed Stuart to climb into the trunk. With Stuart cramped into the trunk of the car, Richard and I never gave it a thought that Stuart could have gotten injured!

We drove for about two miles. I was concerned, so I stopped the car. What would happen if we had a car accident? The trunk might pop open and a policeman might pass by us, turn around and question us. I could have received a traffic ticket or even end up in jail. I insisted that Stuart get out of the trunk. Richard agreed! We blindfolded him and we had him sit in the back seat of the car. Stuart had no idea that we were in Canada. With Stuart blindfolded, sitting in the back seat, we continued our drive to Sherkston Beach which was forty-five miles from the Peace Bridge. There were no other people on Sherkston Beach because it was 2:00 AM. We drove toward the beach; there was a steep sand hill; stepped on the gas pedal pushing down as hard as I could to assure that we would have enough speed to get over the hill.

We were almost at the top when the wheels started to spin; they kept spinning. The car didn't move; we were stuck in the sand. We escorted Stuart out of the car; toward the back. We put his hand on the back of the car and we told him to push. He was still blindfolded! We didn't want Stuart to know where we were. He may have recognized Sherkston Beach because we had a fraternity beach party there the previous week. Richard told Stuart that we were stuck in sand so he would have to push the car. I drove the car. Richard sat in the front passenger seat. Stuart pushed! I looked into my rear view mirror. I did not see Stuart. Richard and I were convinced that Stuart ran away.

We got out of the car and walked toward the back. We did not see Stuart until we looked down. We couldn't stop chuckling. The chuckling became laughter. The laughter became louder laughter. Stuart, still blindfold was lying flat on the ground with his face in the sand. We helped Stuart get up and we removed the blindfold. He was a good sport! Richard helped Stuart push the car out of the sand. The car rolled backward down the hill. We decided that we would tell Stuart where we were because he was such a good sport.

As we drove away, Richard yelled out of the open window "find your own way home". Certainly, Stuart would not be able to brag that he was smarter than all of the fraternity brothers now that he had experienced that episode. We arrived home at 5:00 AM. Richard and I were sitting in the lobby of the dormitory telling our hilarious story to several fraternity brothers. Everyone laughed. Stuart would be embarrassed to walk on campus.

Saul came through the front door. He asked why we were laughing. We told him the story. Saul said that Stuart would have the last laugh because he had arrived in the dormitory one-half hour earlier. Stuart never told anyone how he beat Richard and me home!

I commended him for beating us home. I wasn't upset that he beat us. I was upset that he never stopped bragging about it. The following semester Stuart was no longer a pledge. He was inducted into Pi Epsilon Alpha. He became a fully fledged fraternity Brother. Whenever we were in a room with a group of people he bragged about beating Richard and me home. He was very obnoxious when he bragged.

Stuart didn't realize that "PAY BACK IS A BITCH". I set him up on a DATE WITH JAMIE!

CHAPTER XX

JODIE SUMMERVILLE

J odie Summerville was naïve. I asked her to take a two hours hot air balloon ride with me. The launch pad was in Syracuse NY, approximately a two and one-half hour drive from Buffalo to Syracuse on the NYS Thruway. The touchdown pad was in Binghamton, NY. The drive was approximately four hours from Binghamton to Buffalo. The balloon ride was scheduled for approximately two hours. She didn't do the math! That was certainly going to be an overnight stay.

I told her that I was going to wear a bathing suit and I suggested that she wear a bikini because we were going to be close enough to the sun to get a nice tan. She bought it!

We arrived in Syracuse in mid-afternoon on Saturday. The hot air balloon pilot gave us a few instructions to control the balloon in case something was to happen to him. We weren't concerned. What could possibly happen?

The pilot explained that the hot air balloon consists of a bag known as an envelope that is capable of containing heated air. Suspended beneath is a gondola or wicker basket large enough to hold four people standing or one person standing and two people lying down close to each other. Heated air inside the envelope makes the balloon buoyant. Sand bags attached to the sides of the basket kept the balloon from rising. The pilot would drop the sand bags and increase the fire to fly the balloon.

We were about ready to depart. Jodie and I were standing on one side of the basket. The pilot came to our side and he detached the sand bags. He walked around the basket and detached all of the sand bags. He reached the opposite side of the basket from which we stood. He leaned over to detach the last two bags of sand. The hot air balloon rose approximately three feet; a strong wind blew the pilot out of the basket,

Jodie and I panicked. The balloon kept rising. There was no one to stop the ascent of the balloon. I remembered the pilot's instructions. I lowered the fire from the basket to the balloon. We remained at the same altitude, about eight hundred feet above the ground.

The ride was very smooth and it was very quiet as we floated above the trees. I stopped panicking; I held Jodie tight to calm her. She asked me to hold her tighter. She stopped panicking. She squeezed her breasts together with her arms. I had no idea why she did that. Perhaps she was cold and thought that it would warm her. Jodie's cleavage formed a perfect line between her breasts.

The westerly wind moved the balloon further east away from Syracuse. I knew how to control the ascent and descent; I could not control the wind direction. Jodie turned around to watch the sun begin to set in the west. She asked me to undo the strap on the top of her bikini. She wanted to get the last few rays of sun to tan her already bronze body before the sun settled. She did not want to get tan lines from her bikini top. I accommodated her.

The wind changed its course and the balloon headed west toward Syracuse, our city of origination. I knew that we had a few hours before we would reach Syracuse. I would have to start to lower the balloon. All I would have to do was lower the fire that kept the balloon afloat. I cupped Jodie's breasts. Her back was pressed against my chest.

The sun was settling faster and the temperature began to drop. She turned around to face me and she softly kissed my lips. Jodie lowered her body as she pulled me with her toward the floor of the basket. She thought it would be warmer on the floor with the sides of the basket protecting us from the wind. We were lying on the floor. My chest was firmly against her body, leaving just enough room to place my hands on her breasts. I softly caressed her and circled my finger around her kinipple. We didn't need a space heater. Although there was no warmth from the sun, our bodies burned with desire to keep us warm. However, she would not let me remove the bottom of her bikini. She changed her position and rolled onto her stomach. There was a rectangular clear plastic window on the floor of the basket.

Jodie saw a large sign on the ground 400 feet below us. She read it to me. "WELCOME TO SYRACUSE HOT AIR BALLOON CENTER". We both got off the floor. I lowered the fire and the balloon started its descent. Before we reached the ground, Jodie dressed completely. We raced to the car. She complained that she was cold. I told her that I had a solution. I opened the trunk of the car; and I pulled out a blanket and wrapped it around her body.

It was 2:30 AM. I told Jodie that it would be a two and one-half hour drive from Syracuse to Buffalo. To my pleasant surprise, Jody suggested that we stay in a hotel for the night. I agreed! We drove for a half hour. There were no hotel rooms available so we kept driving until we approached a red blinking sign that read "OPEN". It was a dingy motel. I pulled into the driveway Jodie winked at me and she went to the open window on the side of the building. She spoke to the night clerk. She returned to the car and told me that the rate was $38 per night. She bargained with the clerk. I don't know what she promised him because he lowered the rate to $29 cash including tax.

We entered the dimly lit room. The small double size bed was unmade. There was only one soiled towel hanging from the shower door. Jodie and I shuttered with disgust. She would not take my blanket off her body. In fact she wrapped it tighter. I prayed that there were no bed bugs. Neither one of us slept a wink. It wasn't because we made love; we didn't! Guess who didn't become a Fountain Pen that night!

We decided to drive back to Buffalo that night. I left her off at her dormitory room. She kissed me goodnight and asked me to call her on the phone. I got home fifteen minutes later and I called her on the phone. She laughed as she slammed the phone down!

The next day Jodie called me on the phone to apologize for slamming the phone onto the hook. She had not expected me to call that same night. Most guys would have waited at least one week.

She did want to go on another date with me. I told her that I would definitely call her back in a few days.

The following Friday night we went on a dinner date. We ate hot dogs, fries and a drink. We joked about the pilot falling out of the hot air balloon basket and the dingy motel. She said that she did enjoy the evening.

We were waiting for the waitress to bring the check so we kept joking about that evening. I joked about the size of her tiny breasts. I told her that I would phone her for another date.

I didn't know why she said "DON"T BOTHER!" Of course I never saw her again.

CHAPTER XXI

SAMANTHA FLICKSTEIN

One afternoon, during the winter of 1966, my fraternity brother Mort Gluckburg had a terrible automobile accident. He had been drinking alcohol at the Coconut Shell Tavern on Virginia Street in downtown Buffalo. He became drunk and he decided to drive himself home. Mort crashed into a tree and was taken by ambulance to Millard Fillmore Gates Hospital. He had broken a few bones and he had to stay in the hospital a few days. I went to visit him in the hospital. There were several people visiting him at the same time.

Samantha Flickstein approached me and introduced herself. She was the President of SADD (Students against Drunk Driving); she knew Mort so she visited to console him and discuss the benefits of joining SADD. Mort joined the organization and he stopped drinking entirely. Samantha was a very good looking girl with ash blonde color hair and nicely proportion body. She gave me her phone number. I called her the following week. We decided to take a drive to Crystal Beach because I told her that it was beautiful that time of the year with the snow on the trees and on the cottages. I told her that I had to check on my parent's cottage to make sure that there was no damage from a heavy snow storm the previous month. Samantha was more than willing to go with me.

It was a forty-five minute drive from her dormitory room at SUNY College of Buffalo on Elmwood Avenue to Crystal Beach.

The cottage was boarded up for the winter. I had put a screwdriver, hammer and flashlight into the trunk of the car so that I could get into the cottage.

The cottage was in the middle of a steep hill on Elmwood Avenue in Crystal Beach. On our drive down the hill, toward the cottage, the car slid on an ice patch and at the bottom of the hill, ended up in a ditch. Fortunately for us, a policeman drove by and called for a tow truck to get us out of the ditch. The policeman told the tow truck driver to follow him and to tow the car to the police station. Three people could sit across the front seat of the tow truck.

Samantha sat next to the "grungy looking" driver. She cringed as the man reached for the stick shift which was close to her left leg. Samantha sat as close to me as she could, I paid the driver $10 after he unhooked the car. It was only 9:00 PM so Samantha and I decided to drive the short distance back to the cottage.

I went to the trunk of the car and I grabbed the screwdriver, hammer and flashlight. I knew that the electricity was not turned on inside the cottage so I knew that I would need the flashlight. I used the hammer and screwdrivers to pry open the sheet of plywood that covered the front door.

Fortunately, I remembered to bring the inside front door key. I opened the door. The inside of the cottage was dark so I turned on the dimly lit flashlight. It was the same Dick Tracy flashlight that I used to read "playboy Magazine when I was younger. I escorted Samantha toward the bedroom with the queen size bed. She was not happy that the moth balls were scattered on the bed sheet. I went to the linen closet, removed the moth balls from the sheets and bedspreads and I covered the bed with the "new" sheets and blanket. It was chilly in the room so we left our clothes on our bodies as we crawled under the blanket.

Samantha was as eager as I to start kissing and caressing. That warmed our cold bodies. I unbuttoned her blouse and she unbuttoned my shirt. Our bodies did get warmer. I slipped the blouse off her body.

A bright light shined in the room; a voice yelled "what's going on in here?" It was the same policeman that helped us when we were stuck in the ditch! I had forgotten to bring the plywood board into the cottage and shut the front door. He must have noticed the open door. The policeman accepted my weak explanation that I was checking the cottage for water damage. He let us off easy with a warning. He explained that although it was my parent's cottage, he could have arrested us for breaking and entering. I was upset that he prevented me from becoming a Fountain Pen.

I stood out in the cold putting the plywood board back on the cottage. We drove back to Buffalo. When we reached her dormitory she gave me a short kiss on the lips and asked to go on another date with me. That was a good sign. However, I did have to promise that it would not be at the cottage!

That summer I had remembered Samantha's offer so I phoned her for a date. We drove to Crystal Beach because I told her how beautiful it was with the trees in full bloom and no snow to be seen. I promised that we would not go to the cottage.

One of my favorite places in Crystal Beach was called the B&B Restaurant. The Swing In was no longer open for business. The B&B was located on the same road as the one that leads into Sherkston Beach. It featured greasy hamburgers, French fries with gravy and thick chocolate, vanilla or strawberry milkshakes. I don't remember ever ordering anything else there. We reached the restaurant and the place was dark inside. Too bad it was no longer in business. Samantha would have enjoyed it. We drove to Sherkston Beach. It was originally a stone quarry before it filled with water. There was an old abandoned railroad and the frame of a house at the bottom of the man-made lake. We rented snorkel equipment. I was nervous as I put on the flippers and mask. She wasn't nervous. I was scared as I dove below the surface of the water and touched the slimy seaweed that was attached to the frame of the house. To swim at Sherkston you had to be a good swimmer because the water became deep close to the shoreline. There was a sudden drop off, so you had to be careful in the water. There was a raft that everyone enjoyed swimming to and diving off. Samantha and I swam to the raft. We didn't mind that other people surrounded us as we lay on our backs with our bodies touching; enjoying the hot rays of the sun. It was better than the cold damp cottage in the winter. Nothing else happened!

I didn't only gain a girl friend; I gained a friend, Samantha.

I reminisced about my childhood and I shared my thoughts with Samantha.

I told Samantha about how we took the Canadiana when I was younger. It was a small ferry boat that brought passengers from the foot of Main Street, in Buffalo, to the Crystal Beach Amusement Park.

Everyone disembarked the Canadiana at the Pier that was adjacent to the Amusement Park. The sands of Crystal Beach were to the left and the Amusement Park was to the right as they walked from the Pier to the Park. Samantha and I did many activities together; some were romantic, many were not. It didn't matter. It was more important that we were there for each other as friends. I took Samantha to the Crystal Beach Amusement Park. We walked through the Amusement Park; I pointed out the amusements as I had experienced them as a child. My first "experience" was at a portion of the Park known as Kiddies' Land. I used to ride the kiddies roller coaster, which at that time, was certainly fast enough for me. I was told that the back "car" could come off the tracks. Needless to say, I never sat in the back. The boats floating in, maybe two feet of water, went around and around in a circle. My brother Barney and I would argue over who would sit in the front seat or the back seat of each boat; Even though there were bells to ring and a steering wheel to turn in both the front and the back seats. My sister Marissa always sat next to me in the back seat and Barney sat alone in the front seat. The caterpillar (bug) was a neat, slow moving roller coaster ride with "cars" that looked like their namesake. The Ferris wheel couldn't have been more than 10 feet at its highest point; I am not sure whether adults were allowed to ride on it. The horses on the merry-go-round were not built for adults to sit on. I am sure that there were other rides but I can't remember their names. Next to Kiddies' Land was the "large" merry-go-round. Marissa and I were not allowed to go on it unless a grownup held onto us as it went around in a circle with music playing. It was a lot more exciting than the rides in Kiddies' Land.

As we grew older we "graduated" to the rides in the grownup part of the amusement park and we were allowed to go by ourselves. There was a huge statue of Paul Bunyan at the entrance to the "grownup" portion of the park. We rode on the Giant Yellow roller coaster and the very high, fast and scary roller coaster known as the Comet. The Ferris wheel was very high; the highlight of the ride was to get "stuck" at the top while passengers directly below on the ground level were getting off the ride. The sky ride was exciting as you sat with your feet dangling as the "cars" that were attached to a cable rode over Lake Erie and the sands of Crystal Beach. Of course there were the Pony Rides, Laugh in the Dark and a train ride that circled the outside of the Park. The Magic Carpet was fun. As you walked inside toward the end of the ride (the magic carpet), there were holes in the floor in which puffs of air would raise skirts and pant legs, alike; there were distorted mirrors that made you look tall and thin or short and fat . There were games; which it seemed you could never win, a rifle range with moving ducks, balloons to be broken with darts, bowling pins to be knocked over with a baseball, a duck "pond" in which you picked up out of the water to win a prize, among several other games. I remember the crowds of people, as well as myself staring and enjoying the laughter of "Laughing Sally, a large "figure" located on the left side of the Laughing in the Dark ride. Big Bands played at the Crystal Ballroom for the pleasure of adults to dance. As best as I can remember, children could sneak a peek inside the Ballroom, but were not allowed in. We ate cotton candy, deep-fried waffles coated with powdered sugar; popcorn, hot dogs and fries; Non-carbonated Loganberry or orange were the drinks. Everyone laughed at the sign that read "SUCKERS" as you left the Park. The Crystal Beach suckers were the best (cinnamon, butterscotch, peanut and lemon) with bees swarming around; I always wondered how many times the ladies selling the suckers got stung by the bees. The price of the Freizeitpark tickets was 10 cents and then 35 cents each. We always made sure that we went to the amusement park on the last day of summer before it closed; it was "Nickel Day"; each ticket was only a nickel on that day.

The Four *Mensche* and One Nudnik, Richard, Jacob, Saul, Frankie and I remained friends throughout undergraduate school.

Samantha and I continued our friendship until the day that Frankie embarrassed her and called her a "frigid" tease. I had never confided with him about my relationship with Samantha so I had no idea why he said that to her. Perhaps Richard told him; I always confided with him. On that day, I lost three friends, Samantha, Richard and Frankie. I refused to speak to Richard and Frankie; Samantha refused to speak to me.

CHAPTER XXII

JANE SMYTHE

Saul introduced me to Jane Smythe, a graduate from Gezunt College (GC). GC is a four year college in Buffalo, She was 6'1" tall, slender and she had very broad shoulders and a flat chest, I was able to determine that she lifted weights because of her physical features which included muscular arms and legs. Her brown hair was very short. She had bangs cut straight across her forehead.

Jane was an Aerospace Major. She had high aspirations of becoming an Astronaut. We dated a few times. I enjoyed her sense of humor and many stories about the aerospace program. More importantly, she was strong enough to protect me from anyone that wanted to do me harm! However, she was a bit strange. She challenged my friends and me to arm wrestle and she enjoyed female mud wrestling, which at times, she joined and never lost a match.

Jane had several hours of flight experience; she had a pilot's license. One day she invited me to join her; she had just learned how to fly a plane that featured auto pilot. Our itinerary was Buffalo to Pittsburgh, PA. I relaxed when we were in the air for approximately one-half hour. We talked about American politics and the importance of television and movie influences on American history; she especially respected the influences of the Three Stooges, Little Rascals, Charlie Chaplin and Ronald Reagan.

Jane put the plane into auto pilot and challenged me to arm wrestle. She won the first match. I requested another match. I suggested that the loser of the best two out of three would buy lunch. She won all three. I would have to buy lunch when we landed. . She took the plane out of auto control and she showed me sharp left turns, right turns and straight ascents, our bodies were perpendicular to the back of the plane.

She was not ready to return to Buffalo so she flew the plane to Syracuse. I saw the sign "WELCOME TO SYRACUSE HOT AIR BALLOON CENTER". Jane asked me if I would want to go on a Hot Air Balloon ride, I graciously declined. We continued on our flight, passing over Canandaigua Lake, Ontario Lake and Rochester, NY. She passed over Buffalo and headed toward Toronto, Ontario, Canada.

I asked her whether or not it was legal to fly over Canada. She told me not to worry as she put the plane into auto pilot again. She stood up and started to unbutton her outfit. I was becoming anxious. She was standing in the cramped cockpit completely naked. I was amazed. Her muscles were larger than her miniscule breasts. She "commanded" me to get undressed. I could feel my *schmeckle* enlarge and my groin get warmer. I queried to myself; "were we going to "do it" in the pilot's or co-pilot's seat, there was no space on the floor?" Was I finally going to be a Fountain Pen? I stood up and started to undress. I had taken my shirt and slacks off my body. The weather became bad. The plane took a slight dive. It bounced up and down, side to side.

Jane was completely naked. I was in my boxer shorts. She told me to sit down; she had to take the plane out of auto pilot and she had to take control. She turned the plane around and we headed back to Buffalo. I did not become a Fountain Pen.! We landed at the Buffalo Airport. I put my shirt and pants on my body. She put on her clothes as rapidly as possible. I could see the frustration in her eyes that we did not have sex. I was frustrated too. I had "blue balls"!

I drove Jane to her apartment on the second floor of a four floor apartment building. She asked me to come up for coffee. I graciously refused. She asked me to take another flight someday. I graciously refused. She reached out to hold me. I thought that she was going to slam me down to the floor; she was certainly strong enough! I hurriedly turned around; I slipped on the top step and I slid all the way down to the bottom of the stairway. My *tush* ached as I stood up and ran away as fast as possible. I never saw Jane again.

CHAPTER XXIII

WHITE WATER RAFTING

S aul, Jacob and I went white water rafting one weekend during spring vacation in our junior year at UB. We drove 4 ½ hours to Ohiopyle, Pa. The weekend cost us $100 each which included two breakfasts, one lunch, one dinner and the raft excursion.

At 10:00 PM Friday night we arrived at "Laugh- in-the Face Camp Resort". We drove into the long driveway that led to a large dark brown log cabin. It was the check-in center/dining hall.

The entire "All-Inclusive Resort" consisted of the check-in center/ dining hall, 12 small log cabins and an outdoor 12'X12'swimming pool. The dining hall was attached behind the check-in center. Saul parked the car; Jacob and I paid the desk clerk $300 for the entire weekend package for the three of us. The clerk gave us a flashlight and a skeleton key for cabin #12. It was located in the back of the "resort" amongst a dark thick forest of trees.

A pathway made of a mixture of mud and stone led to our cabin. Saul and Jacob carried the drab green army duffle bags. I carried the toilet paper. I checked out the cabin.

Our cabin had one small bathroom with a shower, toilet and sink. It's a good thing that we brought our own towels and toilet paper. The living room had one lamp with a 40 watt bulb, one wooden chair and a small couch that could seat 1 ½ people. The dark brown logs were exposed; they were the walls .A moose head and a rabbit head were mounted to the wall on the right side of the room. There was no carpet covering the plywood subfloor.

There were three bedrooms. Two bedrooms had one double size bed, one small chair, no dresser and no closet. The third bedroom had one single size bed, one small chair, one night table, no dresser and no closet. The sub plywood floors were covered with red and grey checkered linoleum.

It was 10:45 PM when we completed unpacking. We folded our clothes neatly and put them on the linoleum floor in the third bedroom. It was the cleanest space available. There were no dressers or closets.

The dining hall was closed and the desk clerk was nowhere to be found. Saul suggested that we drive ½ mile down the road. He saw a local bar for us to go for a drink and a snack.

'Gustaf's Bar & Grill" was written on the dirty blue and red blinking neon sign that was in front of the dark green moldy Log Cabin building. We walked inside the dimly lit room. There were three middle age women playing ping pong.

Saul approached the red head that was holding the paddle. She was wearing an orange bowling shirt. "Gustaf's Bar & Grill was embroidered in dark blue thread on the back. Her name "Imogene" was stitched in dark blue thread on the front pocket.

He bet her that he could beat her two out of three games. The woman laughed as she told him that she was the Ohiopyle Ping Pong Champion. He winked at Jacob and me as he grabbed a paddle.

The loser would pay for a drink of the winner's choice. Abigail had unkempt sandy blonde hair. She whispered into Jacob's ear and wagered him that if Imogene won, he would buy the three women two rounds of beer. If Saul won the three women would come back to our cabin and party. Her friend Della agreed to the bet.

Saul won the first two games. He went up to the bartender who was wearing dirty blue jeans and a green and black colored plaid shirt. Saul ordered a dry martini with a lime, two grapes and no ice. The bartender reached under the counter and pulled out a red "Mr. Boston Bartender Guide". He had no idea how to make a dry martini! Saul gulped down the drink as fast as possible. We were anxious to get back to the cabin before the women would change their minds.

The three women, Saul, Jacob and I flipped a coin to determine who would get the room with the single bed; the other two would share the room with the two double beds. I 'm not sure whether I won or lost; I had the single bed. Abigail and Jacob scurried into one of the double beds. Imogene and Saul jumped into the other double bed.

Della told me to get into bed; she had to prepare for the night; I should wait; she would not take a long time. I undressed and I impatiently waited for her in the single bed. I wasn't sure who would sleep on top. The bed was certainly not wide enough for us to sleep side by side.

Saul, Imogene, Jacob and Abigail were noisily romping in the room next to mine.

I was lying on my back. The room was very dark; the only thing I could see was a silhouette of Della standing in the doorway. She was not curvaceous. In fact her body was shaped like a pickle barrel. I decided to close my eyes and pretend that I was with Elizabeth Taylor. Della slid into bed with me. She climbed on top of me; her body felt peculiar.

I opened my eyes; it wasn't Elizabeth Taylor. It was Della, fully clothed. I jumped out of bed, slipped on my pants and went out the door to sleep on a lounge outside by the swimming pool. I did not become a Fountain Pen! I could not sleep a wink. Della came outside. I shined the flashlight in her face and she smiled although she was crying. Della was missing her lower two front teeth and upper left eye tooth.

Got tsu Gaten; nothing happened that night; she was very *mieskeit*! I was actually glad that I did not become a Fountain Pen that night.

I assumed that she was crying because I left her alone in the dark room. I was wrong. She told me she stubbed her toe getting out of bed.

The women left at 7:00 AM that morning. Saul, Jacob and I ate breakfast in the dining hall. We couldn't believe the amount of food that was served. I ate a stack of five pancakes, bacon, cheese omelets, rye toast, coffee, assorted pastries and *kishka*.

After breakfast, we drove to the entrance of "Fast Camp Rapid Tours" to start our venture. To my dismay, Imogene, Abigail and Della arranged with Saul and Jacob to join us white water rafting. We met at the entrance.

We did pay $10 extra to rent rubber wet suits. The guide gave us instructions on how to paddle the 6 passenger raft. He told us that it doesn't happen often, but if we fall out of the raft, we should try to put our feet in front so that we do not hit our head on the rocks. Lucky for us we rented wet suits because light rain drops began to fall. There was no room for a guide to come in our raft so we were on our own. Jacob and I sat up front, Abigail and Della sat in the middle and Imogene and Saul sat in the back.

The trip down the river started; it was a smooth ride, the currents were not fast. We had traveled approximately 2 miles when the rainfall became heavier. The river began to rise, the current became swifter and the rapids became treacherous. There were rocks on both sides of the raft so it was difficult to maneuver. The raft moved vertically out of the water; then suddenly the front of the raft took a huge dip into the water.

I flew 10 feet into the air and landed feet first into the rapidly flowing river. I panicked because I thought that I would die before I became a Fountain Pen! I remembered that I had to put my feet forward so not to bang my head into the rocks. I could not believe how fast the current was as I started to sink toward the bottom of the river. It was not easy but I was able to maneuver my feet forward. My head popped out of the water so I was able to take a breath of air.

Our raft passed by me. Della, Abigail and Imogene laughed at my predicament. Jacob reached out for me but the raft was floating too fast; he couldn't catch me. Saul screamed "try to grab the raft behind us" I traveled another 300 feet when I began to sink again. The next thing I knew; my feet were out of the water. *Oy vey!* I was going over a waterfall; I flew about 10 feet before I landed in a calm pool of water. I swam a few feet to the shore where Jacob and Saul were waiting in the raft. Abigail, Della and Imogene went with another group of men. Good riddance!

The trip continued for a few more miles in much slower moving rapids. We reached the end of the trip. What we were never told was that we had to carry the rafts above our heads along the banks of the river to the entrance. There was no way to paddle upstream. That's twice that I would go white water rafting; the first and last time.

It was 6:00 PM when we arrived back to the cabin. We missed lunch; we didn't care; we were exhausted! It took about two hours to shower one at a time in cold water. Dinner was going to be served at 8:30 PM, so we made it just in time Again, we were pleasantly surprised! There was a huge buffet of salad, shrimp, crab legs, French onion soup, chicken, steak, lasagna, assorted fruit, assorted desserts and of course, *kishka*.

That evening we went back to "Gustaf". I prayed that Della would not be there. My prayers were answered!

There were three young girls playing billiards.

Saul approached the red head that was holding the cue stick. She was wearing an orange bowling shirt. "Gustaf's Bar & Grill was embroidered in dark blue thread on the back. The name stitched in dark blue thread on the front pocket was "Imogene's Daughter."

He bet her that he could beat her two out of three games. The girl laughed as she told him that she was the Ohiopyle Billiard Champion. He winked at Jacob and me as he grabbed a cue stick.

The loser would pay for a drink of the winner's choice. Abigail's daughter had unkempt sandy blonde hair. She whispered into Jacob's ear and wagered him that if Imogene's daughter won, he would buy the girl's two rounds of beer. If Saul won the three girls would come back to our cabin and party. Her friend Della's daughter agreed to the bet.

Saul won the first two games. He went up to the bartender who was wearing dirty blue jeans and a green and black colored plaid shirt. Saul ordered a Manhattan with a lime, two grapes and no ice. The bartender reached under the counter and pulled out the red "Mr. Boston Bartender Guide". He had no idea how to make a Manhattan! Saul gulped down the drink as fast as possible. We were anxious to get back to the cabin before the girls would change their minds. The girls did change their minds.

Their mothers were waiting for them at Ohiopyle Bowling Lanes. It was Ladies' Night at the Lanes. Della's daughter looked at me and smiled. Her two bottom front teeth and upper left eye tooth were missing. It must have been in the genes or they were in the same fight.

Gustaf Junior, the bartender introduced himself to Saul and told him that it was Men's Night at Gustaf Bar & Grill. Female entertainers were performing at 2:00 AM.

We sat at a table in front of the stage. The Female performers appeared. They were gorgeous. There were six performers; they looked like sisters; all wore gold color wigs, red sequin dresses, long white gloves and purple sequin high heel shoes. The glass pendant on their long gold necklaces fell into the exact same place in the narrow cleavage of their very tiny breasts.

Master of Ceremonies Monique introduced Louise, a songstress from Hungary. She sang two love songs:

"Kiss me on the high cliff" and "Kiss me on the low cliff"

Jonnie, Roxy and Billie were tap dancers; they were so bad that they should not have performed.

Monique went behind the red velvet curtain and came back carrying a chair. She placed the chair on the stage as she introduced Nance, an international "Stand Up" Comic.

Pauli, a ventriloquist held her stuffed pet dragon to perform their act.

The entertainment ended at 3:00 AM. Nance came over to our table and asked if one of us would play ping pong or billiards. She would lay a wager that Pauli and her pet dragon would win both games. The wager was that the loser would buy two rounds of beer for the ladies or two drinks of choice for each of the boys. She forewarned us that Pauli and the dragon were the Ohiopyle runner ups in the Ping Pong and Billiards Championship Tournament.

Saul jumped up without hesitation. Monique whispered into Jacob's ear. "If Saul wins, all six ladies would come to our cabin and party." Saul won all of the games! He walked up to Gustaf Junior and ordered three dry martinis and three Manhattans. Junior reached under the counter and pulled out his red Mr. Boston Bartender's Guide. He had forgotten how to mix the drinks.

Monique, Louise, Pauli with the dragon puppet on her hand walked with us to our cabin. Jonnie, Billie and Roxy hesitated and walked slowly. I walked with them and spoke with the girls about our experience on the river. Roxy said "you haven't experienced anything yet! I was really looking forward to getting back to the cabin with the girls.

Saul hooked up with Pauli and the dragon; that would be interesting. Jacob hooked up with Monique.

I looked backwards over my shoulder; Gustaf Junior was cleaning the dirt laden marquis. I read the sign:
"SPECIAL TONIGHT ONLY
MONIQUE AND HER FEMALE IMPERSONATORS"
I ran like hell back to Gustaf's Bar & Grill. I did not say a word to Saul or Jacob. It wasn't too bad sleeping on the lounge by the side of the swimming pool that night. When I woke up in the morning, Saul and Jacob were standing over me with two buckets of ice water in their hands. They were pissed.

We went to breakfast and we couldn't believe that the amount of food was more than the previous day's breakfast. I ate fruit cocktail a stack of five pancakes, bacon, cheese omelets, steak, rye toast, coffee, assorted pastries and *kishka*. Saul and Jacob didn't say a word about the previous night and I didn't ask!

The drive home was more pleasant than I expected. Saul and Jacob still didn't say a word about the previous night but they did joke about the fact that no one saw the marquis advertising that night's entertainment.

About half way home, Saul noticed a "For Sale" sign on a 1929 convertible "Gazelle" Mercedes Benz in a farmer's driveway. I slammed on the brakes, almost causing a five car crash up. We could certainly negotiate to purchase the car for less than $3,000. How could a farmer know the true value of the antique car?

There was a man dressed in blue bib top over hauls with no shirt. He probably wasn't wearing under clothes either. We walked up to him and we noticed that the barn door was wide open. There were two cars parked inside. The farmer proudly showed us his 1955 red convertible Thunderbird and 1935 two tone black and yellow convertible Stutz Bearcat automobiles. We offered him $3,000 for the Chevrolet. He graciously declined and told us to turn around and leave before he went into the farm house to get his shotgun for wasting his time and insulting him. As we hightailed out of his driveway, he shouted "I'll give you a deal; $125,000 for all three cars".

We heard a loud "bang". I wet my pants, positive that we were going to die. I checked with Saul and Jacob; they were not bleeding; neither was I. The car had back fired!

CHAPTER XXIV

MYSTERY TRIP

S aul planned a special vacation for winter break during our senior year at UB. We convinced three fraternity brothers William, Norbert and Boris to get "dates" and the twelve of us would take a "mystery vacation". Saul told no one where we were going. The vacation was planned to be from a Saturday morning to Sunday morning. Everyone was more than willing to join us.

The only information that Saul gave was that it would be a warm climate area so everyone should pack a bathing suit, toga, sandals and casual clothes. The total cost would be $1,000 per couple. That included airfare, lodging and meals. The only thing not included was alcohol, personal spending money and condoms.

Saul and Roxanne, Jacob and Kate, William and Nancy, Norbert and Velma, Boris and his date; and Samantha and I were eager to vacation as a group. That's correct. I had called Samantha to apologize for our misunderstanding and that I missed her dearly. There was no one else that I would rather share this vacation. Samantha agreed but stated that "sex was off the table". I responded that we "never had sex on a table". She chuckled!

All twelve of us arranged to go Niagara Falls International Airport at 7:00 AM the Saturday that we were leaving for the trip.

Saul and I could not believe our eyes. Jacob told us that Boris' date backed out of the "trip" so he needed to be "fixed" up with a "date". Jacob laughed as he told us that he "fixed" up Boris with Jamie (James). We had to tell everyone where we were going as we passed through TSA inspection to board the airplane. No one was disappointed that we were on our way to Aciamaj Island in the Caribbean Sea.

We disembarked the plane at 3:00 PM. The moment we passed through customs, a small group of native Islanders approached us with plants in their hands. Saul and Jacob bought 16 ounces of marijuana. Saul bragged that they only paid $25 per ounce.

We arrived at Inn o' scent Golf Club Resort at 5:00 PM that Saturday night. Samantha and I checked into our room. Two of the walls were painted orange and two walls were painted yellow. The ceiling was painted light blue with white clouds to give an appearance of the sky. The drapes were orange and yellow stripes to blend with the colors of the walls. The white marble floors had a brown braided throw rug on each side of the bamboo headboard queen size bed. The bathroom had a single sink, bathtub and shower. A bidet was next to the toilet that flushed with a pull chain hanging from the ceiling.

We unpacked the clothes that we had, namely, a few bathing suits, a few casual clothes and two togas.

The first night we all agreed to wear togas. Samantha went into the closet to put on her toga as I dressed in the bedroom. There was no television in the room so I turned on the radio and listened to reggae music. It was agreed by all of us to eat at the open air dining room for dinner at 8:00 PM.

The dining room had a straw thatch ceiling with fans circulating the warm air for ventilation. There were 50 round tables with 12 chairs at each table. The long buffet table was bountiful with assorted salads; fruit: pineapple, watermelon, cantaloupe, grapes, oranges and apples; entrees: pork, chicken, turkey, roast beef and beef stroganoff; dessert was lime pie, coconut pie and soupy ice cream.

Saul and Roxanne, Jacob and Kate, William and Nancy, Norbert and Velma, Boris and Jamie and Samantha and I formed two lines to stroll down an isle to the tune of a "reggae stroll".

All of the girls had cute curvaceous figures dressed in their togas, except Jamie. Her body looked similar to that of the guys. Saul, Jacob, Jamie and I knew why; the others had no clue. After the dancing had finished we all walked to Saul and Roxanne's room to "party". Their room was the largest. Saul, Jacob and I went into the bathroom to roll reefers while our other friends waited impatiently in the bedroom.

We had never smoked marijuana, let alone roll it. It was not easy to roll; we used glue to hold the rolled paper together. Everyone took a "stick" except Samantha and Velma. Jamie laughed out loud as he shouted "this is not marijuana, it is spinach"! What did we know? That was very expensive spinach!

We left the party and sauntered to our rooms. Samantha and I returned to our bedroom and we discussed the day's activities. We were still dressed in our togas, Samantha asked me to hold her tight. It took 30 minutes to fall asleep.

The next morning we awoke at 8:00 AM. Samantha went into the bathroom first to shower. She came out of the bathroom dressed in a pretty pink bikini. I took a shower and put on my knee length black bathing suit. All of the girls wore a bikini except Jamie who wore a one piece dark brown bathing suit.

The same long buffet table included an assortment of breads, rolls, challahs and jams; bacon and eggs and *kishka*. The staff must have forgotten to serve the *kishka* the previous evening at dinner.

The conversation started with laughter about the spinach. Jacob asked Boris about his evening. Boris looked at Jamie, winked and said "very interesting". After breakfast we went to the swimming pool. We basked in the 85 degrees warmth of the orange colored sun high above our heads.

Saul and Roxanne, Jacob and Kate, Norbert and Velma, Samantha and I skipped lunch. Robert and Nancy, Boris and Jamie ate lunch; and decided to play golf after lunch.

We met for dinner at 8:00 PM. After dinner there was a talent contest among the guests of the resort. 11 of us sang Swing Low, Sweet Chariot using hand gestures for each word. The crowd loved it. We came in second place. Velma sang "Over the Rainbow" came in first place and won a free one week vacation at the resort.

The next day we planned an excursion to climb up the Snud River Waterfalls. It was a wonderful experience holding hands to form a human chain to climb up the waterfall. When we reached the top we walked on a path that had several huts on both sides. An island native approached us and offered to sell us marijuana. Not to be duped again, we insisted that Jamie deal with him. After all, she was the only one that knew we rolled spinach the other night. She made the purchase for $10 per ounce.

Another man approached William and offered to sell him a picture of his nude younger sister; William paid 50 cents. Then the man approached Saul and Jacob and offered them the opportunity to *shtoop* his older sister; he would *shtoop* Roxanne and Kate while Saul and Jacob were busy with his sister. They all refused and ran like hell toward our excursion bus.

Safely sitting on the bus, we urged the driver to drive away from the area as fast as possible. After being on the road for about an hour, all of the girls complained that they had to pee. The driver said that the closest rest area was another one hour away. Velma screamed that she could not wait any longer. Roxanne exclaimed" we can stop here"!

The driver slammed on the brakes, opened the bus door and the girls jumped out. They scurried into the sugar cane field. Out of sight from the bus, they all squatted, except for Jamie. Everyone wondered why Jamie didn't squat. The girls boarded the bus and we continued toward the resort.

We arrived at the resort in time for 8:00 PM dinner. The long buffet table had the same selections as the previous night dinner. After dinner, we went to Saul and Roxanne's room. Boris and Jamie rolled the marijuana; Norbert and Kate mixed the Rum and Coke drinks. Within two hours, Norbert became inebriated and stoned. He passed out on the floor. Roxanne insisted that he could not stay in her and Saul's room. Jacob went to the swimming pool area and brought back a lounge chair. We picked up Norbert and we placed him on the lounge chair; carried him across the resort and left him in the empty open air dining room. He was passed out stone cold and never woke up.

The next morning we met in the dining room for breakfast. Norbert was still there asleep on the lounge. The other guests were confused; they whispered to each other, questioning why Norbert was lying on the lounge in the middle of the dining room. Norbert didn't know how he got there!

That afternoon we separated, some sat by the pool, went scuba diving or rented a catamaran. We were concerned that we would have the same experience as the previous night so we flushed the marijuana down the toilet. Without our knowledge Norbert pocketed some of the marijuana. Although none of us drank alcohol, Norbert did drink. He got drunk and decided to go to his room with Velma to sleep it off.

The vacation ended on the following Sunday, we boarded the plane and returned to UB. Graduation was in June. Everyone graduated except Norbert. Sadly, he became an alcoholic and drug addict. He was in rehab and he missed graduation.

Samantha enrolled at John Hopkins University and became a well respected neurologist.

Saul graduated and became a travel agent.

Jacob graduated and developed an e-commerce dating business.

William graduated and went to acting school. He was never in a feature role.

Velma graduated and became a well known songstress, was the lead singer for a famous rock band, married and divorced within one year.

Boris and James joined a female impersonator troupe.

I graduated and became a government agent; I can not disclose which agency.

CHAPTER XXV

FINALLY, I BECAME A FOUNTAIN PEN

At the Agency I met Selma, a beautiful blonde, thin waste and large breasts, of course. She was 5'9". I was shorter, standing 5'7". I was 24 years old; she was 23. We became engaged and we went to Niagara Falls, New York to celebrate our engagement. The first night we made passionate love. Finally, I became a Fountain Pen!

The next day she left me and ran away with a 19 year old boy. I never saw her again!

THE END

Printed in the United States
By Bookmasters